P9-CFS-869

THE CLUES

As he turned to go, Meat noticed a lipstick halfway between where he had found the wallet and the door to one of the stalls. He didn't pick this up. He just stared at it as if trying to make a connection.

The wallet...

The lipstick...

His eyes continued to look.

A hair brush—a dainty one with speckles like confetti in the plastic.

The objects began to take on the feeling of a trail, things leading to something.

And Meat knew that at the end of the trail there was going to be something he didn't like.

Something that would change his life.

And not for the better.

"Readers should be prepared to read this in one breathless sitting."
—*School Library Journal*

BOOKS BY BETSY BYARS

The Herculeah Jones Mysteries:
The Dark Stairs
Tarot Says Beware
Dead Letter
Death's Door
Disappearing Acts
King of Murder

The Bingo Brown books:
Bingo Brown, Gypsy Lover
Bingo Brown and the Language of Love
Bingo Brown's Guide to Romance
The Burning Questions of Bingo Brown

Other titles:
After the Goat Man
The Cartoonist
The Computer Nut
Cracker Jackson
The Cybil War
The 18th Emergency
The Glory Girl
The House of Wings
McMummy
The Midnight Fox
The Summer of the Swans
Trouble River
The TV Kid

DISAPPEARING ACTS

District Reading
Adoption

A HERCULEAH JONES MYSTERY

DISAPPEARING ACTS

BY BETSY BYARS

SLEUTH
PUFFIN

PUFFIN BOOKS

Published by the Penguin Group

Penguin Young Readers Group, 345 Hudson Street, New York, New York 10014, U.S.A.

Penguin Group (Canada), 90 Eglinton Avenue East, Suite 700, Toronto, Ontario, Canada M4P 2Y3
(a division of Pearson Penguin Canada Inc.)

Penguin Books Ltd, 80 Strand, London WC2R 0RL, England

Penguin Ireland, 25 St Stephen's Green, Dublin 2, Ireland (a division of Penguin Books Ltd)

Penguin Group (Australia), 250 Camberwell Road, Camberwell, Victoria 3124, Australia
(a division of Pearson Australia Group Pty Ltd)

Penguin Books India Pvt Ltd, 11 Community Centre, Panchsheel Park, New Delhi - 110 017, India

Penguin Group (NZ), Cnr Airborne and Rosedale Roads, Albany, Auckland 1310, New Zealand
(a division of Pearson New Zealand Ltd)

Penguin Books (South Africa) (Pty) Ltd, 24 Sturdee Avenue, Rosebank,
Johannesburg 2196, South Africa

Registered Offices: Penguin Books Ltd, 80 Strand, London WC2R 0RL, England

First published in the United States of America by Viking,
a division of Penguin Books USA Inc., 1998
Published by Puffin Books, 2000
This Sleuth edition published by Puffin Books, a division of Penguin Young Readers Group, 2006

5 7 9 10 8 6 4

Copyright © Betsy Byars, 1998
All rights reserved

THE LIBRARY OF CONGRESS HAS CATALOGED THE VIKING EDITION AS FOLLOWS:

Byars, Betsy Cromer.
Disappearing Acts / by Betsy Byars.
p. cm.—(A Herculeah Jones mystery)
Summary: Herculeah stumbles onto the trail of her friend Meat's long-lost father
while she and Meat are investigating the disappearance of a dead
body from the men's room of a comedy club.
ISBN: 0-670-87735-2 (hc)
[1. Fathers and sons—Fiction. 2. Mystery and detective stories.]
I. Title. II. Series: Byars, Betsy Cromer. Herculeah Jones mystery.
PZ7.B9836Di 1998 [Fic]—dc21 97-29434 CIP AC

Puffin Books ISBN 0-14-240566-3

Printed in the United States of America

Except in the United States of America, this book is sold subject to the condition that
it shall not, by way of trade or otherwise, be lent, re-sold, hired out, or otherwise
circulated without the publisher's prior consent in any form of binding or cover
other than that in which it is published and without a similar condition
including this condition being imposed on the subsequent purchaser.

The publisher does not have any control over and does not assume
any responsibility for author or third-party Web sites or their content.

CONTENTS

1. Herculeah on the Run   1
2. To Die Laughing   5
3. A Premonition   11
4. Missing Person   15
5. The Guy-ette   21
6. Stage Fright   25
7. The Busy Body   29
8. The Olympic Scream   35
9. Proof Positive   39
10. Name of the Game   44
11. Nineteen Exposures   49
12. Meat on His Own   55
13. Bad News   63
14. Unlucky Seven   67
15. The Message   71
16. A Body in the Closet   74
17. Phone Call   79
18. The Face in the Crowd   82
19. The Smile on the Crocodile   89
20. Herculeah's Hair   96
21. A Stab in the Dark   98
22. Macho Man   102
23. The Earthquake   106
24. The Gotta-Go Gene   113
25. The Next Mystery   116

CONTENTS

1

HERCULEAH ON THE RUN

April Fools' Day started with a pretend murder and ended with a real one.

It was Saturday morning, ten o'clock, and Herculeah Jones came around the corner, fast. Her hair flew out behind her as she ran.

Meat was sitting on his front porch. He had been watching for Herculeah, smiling in anticipation of telling her his big news. As soon as he saw her, he stood and moved to the steps.

Herculeah glanced toward him.

Meat saw her expression. There was something in her face, her manner, that instantly alarmed him. His smile of anticipation faded.

He checked to see if her hair was frizzing. Herculeah had what he called radar hair. It reacted to danger like an animal's fur. It got bigger.

At that moment, Herculeah's hair did look bigger than normal, and that increased his feeling of dread.

He hesitated, and then hurried down the steps. "What happened?" he called.

Herculeah didn't answer. She waved him off with her arm as if she didn't have time to stop.

Meat hurried across the street, not even pausing to check for traffic.

"What is it? What's happened?"

"Meat—" But she was too out of breath to continue. She pressed the fingers of one hand into her side.

"What?"

"Meat—"

"What? What? I can't stand this. What's happened? Don't do this to me!"

She looked at him with her clear gray eyes. They seemed darker now. Meat thought that could be because they were clouded with fear.

"What?"

"A body," she managed to say.

Meat took a step backward. He put one hand over his heart.

"Not again?"

She nodded.

"Dead?"

Again Herculeah nodded.

"Killed?"

Another nod. Meat felt as if he were trying to communicate with one of those dashboard animals that can't do anything but nod.

"Where?"

"Oak."

"Oak Street?"

"Yes."

"Herculeah, this is your third dead body!"

"I know."

He began to count them. "Old man Crewell . . . Madame Rosa—and I could have been the third! Remember the Bull!"

"I remember." She gave a helpless sigh. "I don't want to find dead bodies. I can't help it."

He watched her and then he sighed too, as if accepting the unfortunate fact.

"Male or female?"

"I couldn't tell."

Meat's hand over his heart tightened so that he clutched his shirt.

"Mutilated?"

"Badly."

"Don't tell me any details." Meat began to feel a little sick. "I don't want to hear any details." He held up his hand as if to ward them off. "Whatever you do, don't give me details."

"Just one."

"Is it gory?"

"A little."

"Then I don't want to hear it! No! I'll have bad dreams. I'm going to put my fingers in my ears."

"I'm sorry. You have to hear this."

Meat waited.

Herculeah smiled.

"The body was a squirrel on Oak Street. A car ran over it. April Fool!"

2

TO DIE LAUGHING

Meat's expression went from concern to fury in one second. "That is not funny," he sputtered. "That is really not funny."

"Oh, come on, admit it. It was a little bit funny."

"Maybe to you. To me, jokes like that are sick!"

"Don't be mad at me."

"I am. I can't help it. I was having this wonderful day—and I don't have them that often—and you spoil it with a sick joke about finding a body."

"Come on it. I'll make you popcorn. Will you forgive me for popcorn?"

Meat hesitated. "No," he decided. "I'm getting ready to begin a new life tonight—"

"Oh, I almost forgot." Herculeah pulled a small camera from her pocket. "Smile!"

Meat's frown deepened.

Click.

"Why did you do that? You know I hate to have my picture taken. You're deliberately trying to irritate me— and you're succeeding!"

"Meat, listen," she said, her tone softening. "I bought this camera at Hidden Treasures. I don't know why I even went in there. I only had one dollar, and nothing in there costs one dollar."

Meat waited.

"I was drawn to the "As Is" table—all items as is. There was something about this table that bothered me. Some of the things were familiar, but . . . but I don't know from where. Anyway, as soon as my hand touched the camera, my hair began to frizz."

"But why would you pick up something that could put you in danger?"

"A camera? A camera's dangerous? Be real. Anyway," she paused to advance the film, "there was a roll of film in the camera and five exposures left. I want to finish the roll. Smile!"

Click.

"I'm going back to my house if you don't put that camera away."

Herculeah took his arm. "Did you say something about starting a new life?"

"Yes, but you don't want to hear about it."

"I do."

"You'd rather play stupid tricks on people and take pictures."

"Come on, Meat. Popcorn . . . think popcorn."

She drew him into her house, then her kitchen. "Sit," she said, pointing to a chair by the table. Meat sat. Herculeah put popcorn in the microwave, punched in four minutes, and sat across from Meat.

"You have my complete attention," she said. "Tell me about your new life."

Meat wished now that they were back outside. Her eyes were too gray, too piercing. He felt she could see through to his brain.

"Well, you've heard about Funny Bonz?" he began.

"The comedy club? On the corner of Wright and Peachtree?"

"It used to be there. It's moved. It's right up the street now, in the basement of the old hotel."

"I just passed the hotel. I didn't notice any signs."

"Maybe you were too busy looking for dead squirrels. Anyway, they just opened. The club's under new management—a guy named Mike Howard."

"Actually, I'm not that interested in comedy, Meat. I'm not a very funny person."

"Well, nobody's perfect," Meat said generously.

"I come pretty close though, don't I?" She grinned at him.

The silence that followed was broken by the sound of popping corn. Meat's mouth began to water. Herculeah said, "And you're going to the club?"

"Better than that—much better. I'm going to be on the stage of the club! I'm going to perform! I'm going to be a stand-up comic!"

"Meat, you can't." She stared at him in amazement. "You're not any funnier than I am."

"I wouldn't say that." He was obviously offended. "Just because I don't run around playing stupid April Fool jokes on people."

"Meat," she interrupted. "Sometimes you are funny, but it just pops out. It's not planned—like when you were little you wanted someone to write books about the Unhardy Boys."

"I didn't mean that to be funny." Now he was really offended.

"Meat, start over. Please."

"All right. Well, there was this article in the newspaper about the club. It was about how taking lessons in comedy can help people accept themselves. Being funny about yourself is therapeutic."

"I never felt I needed therapy. I do accept myself."

"Well, I don't exactly need therapy either."

The conversation was going downhill from an already low beginning. Fortunately the popcorn was ready, and Meat took a handful.

"You take lessons . . ." Herculeah prompted.

Meat nodded, chewing.

"So there's a class," she went on.

"Yes," he admitted, "there's a class."

"How many students?"

"I don't know. I haven't been there yet. You know, I was all excited about this until you started picking at it. There's even a graduation night when everyone performs. I was going to invite you, but . . ."

"Meat, I have to come!"

He took another handful of popcorn. "No, you'll laugh."

"Meat, that's what I'm supposed to do—laugh!"

"Well, maybe you can come. All we have to do for tonight—it's like an assignment—is make up a joke about ourselves."

"What's yours?"

Meat said, "I don't know. I'd like to do something about not having a father."

"But that's not funny, Meat."

"I know that! But if I could turn it into something funny, well, then maybe it wouldn't hurt so much."

Meat went over the possibilities of all the highlights of his life that his dad missed out on—like what? Like getting an A in spelling in Miss Richard's room?

He paused. What really hurt was that his dad had hardly missed out on anything.

"If that fails, there's always my size," he said glumly. The many possible jokes about that were not appealing. He went over a few to himself.

I'm so big that when I'm around the house, I'm a-r-o-u-n-d the house.

I'm so big I have my own area code.

9

When I put on my blue suit and stand on a corner, people try to drop mail in my mouth.

He had gotten these from a book of fat jokes at the newsstand. He had spent so long leafing through the book, reading the insults without smiling, that the clerk had come over and asked him if he wanted to buy it.

"This? No, this is a terrible book." He had returned it at once to the humor shelf where, in his opinion, it definitely did not belong.

Well, he might have to stop by and refresh his memory if he decided to go that way. Ah, yes, the jokes were coming back to him. Meat had good recall, especially of things he did not want to recall.

When I was lying on the beach, Greenpeace tried to push me back into the water.

He broke off his thoughts and turned to Herculeah. "Well, whatever I do, nobody will die laughing."

Later, that was the remark that Herculeah was to remember.

A remark that would cause her hair to frizzle everytime she heard it.

"Nobody will die laughing."

3

A PREMONITION

"My hair started doing this when I bought the camera,"
Herculeah told her mother. She fluffed out her hair.
"And it won't quit."

Herculeah was sitting at the kitchen table. A slice of
pizza lay untouched on her plate.

Herculeah's mother glanced at her. "You're probably
just having a bad hair day."

"No, when my hair frizzles, it's because of danger. I
know you don't believe it."

"I never said I didn't believe it," her mother answered
carefully. "In fact, I sometimes find myself thinking, 'If I

were Herculeah, my hair would be reaching for the sky right now.'"

"Well, Meat knows it's true. He's seen proof. He's seen it work."

She hesitated.

Her mother watched her, knowing there was more.

"Remember when the Moloch nailed me up in the basement of Dead Oaks? My hair frizzled. Remember when Madame Rosa's murderer was after me? My hair frizzled. And remember—"

Her mother cut her off. "You've made your point."

Herculeah slumped in her chair.

"Maybe it's your imagination this time," her mother suggested.

"How?"

"Well, maybe you expect the things you get at Hidden Treasures to cause you trouble—like Amanda Cole's coat."

Herculeah's expression was serious. "Yes! Mom, you're right! I was drawn to the 'As Is' table in the exact same way I was drawn to that coat. And I just stood there because something about the things on that table bothered me."

"What?"

"I'd seem them before."

"Where?"

"That's what bothered me. I don't know. Anyway, I picked up the camera, and it had been marked down to one dollar—the exact amount I had. I was meant to buy this camera. For some reason that I don't know, I was meant to buy this camera!"

Herculeah turned it over in her hands.

"I wonder," she said thoughtfully, "if it has anything to do with the pictures on the film."

"What pictures?"

"Somebody took nineteen pictures of something—or somebody—and they're still in the camera. Maybe when I see those nineteen pictures, I'll know why I was drawn to the camera. I just wish my hair would stop frizzling."

"Look," her mother said in her sensible voice, "you are sitting in your own kitchen, eating a pizza you made yourself. Where's the danger?"

"I don't know."

Herculeah looked down at the camera beside her plate. "Do you suppose it could be someone else who's in danger?"

"Such as?"

"Oh, I don't know." She smiled. "Well, at least I know it's not Meat."

"Where is Meat?"

"He's at Funny Bonz."

"What's that? A new barbecued ribs place?"

"Oh, Mom. It's a comedy club. Meat's learning to be funny. He's going to take stand-up comic lessons, and I get to go to the graduation."

Her mother smiled. "I hope I can come. I could use a good laugh."

"Me too."

Herculeah tried to smile, but she didn't succeed.

"I know there's more," her mother said. "What else is on your mind?"

"Remember when Meat and I went over to Death's Door to reshelve the books? Remember, after that sniper tipped over the shelves trying to get to me?"

"I remember."

"Well, when we were shelving the books, I picked one up, and you know what the name of it was?"

"I can't imagine."

"*Funny Bones*—like the comedy club—and I got one of my premonitions."

"And I've got one of my premonitions. Your pizza's getting cold."

Herculeah picked up the slice of pizza. "Oh, I wonder what they're doing right now. I wish I could see Meat."

"I thought you weren't worried about Meat."

"I'm not. I just wish I could see him."

"Meat's conservative. He doesn't take chances—not like you do. Meat's always safe."

"Nobody—" Herculeah looked at her mother. Her gray eyes were dark with concern. "*Nobody* is always safe."

4

MISSING PERSON

"We're supposed to have a joke about ourselves," a white-haired woman at the table with Meat told him. They sat side by side at one of the tables at Funny Bonz. "Did you know that?"

"Yes, I heard."

"I asked her," she nodded to the girl across the table, "what hers was. Want to know what she said?"

"I guess."

"She said that everybody tells her she looks like Barbie, then she added, 'Well, I do buy my clothes at Toys "Я" Us.'"

Meat smiled.

"I'm worried. I don't think mine's any good. Can I try it on you?"

"Sure."

"Well, everybody tells me I look like Mrs. Santa Claus, so that's what my joke's about. Here goes." She took a breath. "It's hard living with elves. It's not like Snow White's Dopey and Sneezy. Our elves are Gropey and Sleazy." She gave him a hopeful look. "What do you think?"

Meat was spared having to answer by the arrival of the teacher, a lanky man who was smiling and rubbing his hands together as if he were drying them.

All the students broke into smiles—not because the teacher had said or done anything funny, but in anticipation of the funny things they would all be saying and doing before the night was over.

The teacher, Mike Howard, counted heads and glanced at his watch. "Hey, we're missing one." He glanced around the room. "We'll wait. This is one funny person—just about ready to try the circuit—wanted to sharpen things up a bit."

Meat glanced at the girl across the table. She did have a lot of hair like Barbie. And her clothes did look like they might have some from Toys "Я" Us.

"So what did you think?" Mrs. Santa Claus asked. "About my joke."

While Meat was working up a lie, someone at another table said, "While we're sweating out the absentee, Mike, tell us how you got started."

16

"I thought you'd never ask." He sat on the edge of one of the tables. "I got my start in fourth grade. I had never done one funny thing before, and then one day when the teacher, Miss Parotti, left the room, I was on my way to the pencil sharpener and I stopped at her desk and surprised myself by doing an imitation. 'Boys and girls—' Her nickname, incidentally, was Mush Mouth. 'Boys and girls, will the person who made the bad smell please identify yourself by making another bad smell so that I can send you to the rest room.'"

His imitation of Mush Mouth brought smiles, and Barbie let out a delighted yell: "I think I had her for homeroom."

"So this huge, huge success—the first of my life—led to greater things. Mr. Ledbetter—he was the principal: 'Now boys and girls, I am just getting over my hookworm treatment and . . .'"

Everyone—including Meat—laughed this time, and Mike shook his head at the memory.

"It was instant fame. I mean, kids I'd never seen before would come up to me in the lunch line and say, 'Do my teacher. Please!' I'd go, 'Who is your teacher?' 'Miss Prunty.' 'Right. Boys and girls, will whoever borrowed my book *Laxatives of the Rich and Famous* please return it immediately. I need it before the end of the school day.'"

Mike gave a shrug of apology. Then he added, "They loved it. What can I tell you."

All this bathroom humor made Meat decide to go to one. He didn't really have to go, but when he got up to do a routine—or didn't they do that this early in the lessons? Anyway, he would certainly have to go then.

"Rest rooms?" he asked Barbie.

"I never go," she said.

"I thought you just did," Mrs. Santa Claus said. "You went somewhere."

She shrugged. The man at the next table jabbed his finger toward a dark hall beside the stage.

Meat proceeded slowly toward the unappealing hall, skirting the tables as he went.

Behind him, Mike warmed to his story. "My comedy career lasted about two weeks. Then Mr. Ledbetter called me into his office and asked me to do my impersonation of him. Talk about your hostile audience. Then he asked if I had any other impressions. I did the entire staff, even the cafeteria workers, and he did not crack one smile. Not even at Mrs. Richards—'Will whoever took my Gas-Away tablets please return them, or you will be very, very sorry.'"

Meat had moved out of voice range. The building was old and the hall smelled of disinfectant and urine, as if someone hadn't quite made it to the rest room.

There was graffiti on the walls. Meat paused to read the messages as he walked slowly toward the two doors at the end. "D.J. wanted to call 911; he got the nine right but couldn't find the eleven." "Call Betty for real laughs." Maybe he would dial. He needed a laugh more than he needed a rest room.

Meat was sorry he had come—not just to the rest

room, but to Funny Bonz as well. He had a feeling in his own bonz, and he didn't like it.

To keep up his spirits, he began to whistle. He recognized the song as that old camping song about the worms crawling in and out of a dead person.

At the end of the hall, Meat stopped between the two doors. He always doubled-checked the signs on restroom doors. This was because he had a recurring nightmare of being trapped in the girls' bathroom at school.

He had to peer closely because of the dim light. The sign on the door to the right said "Guys." The sign across the hall said "Guy-ettes."

Herculeah would not like that word "guy-ettes." She didn't even approve of "Guys" and "Dolls." He'd have to warn her before she came to graduation.

He read the signs one more time, just to be sure. They still said the same thing, so Meat, reasonably confident, opened the door to Guys.

The room was darker than the hall, and Meat felt for the light switch.

He turned it on and was almost sorry he had. A roach hurried back to the baseboard. The floor was covered with crumpled paper towels, scraps of toilet paper, and various unidentifiable debris.

The window was open. Meat was grateful for that and for the fresh air that came through it. Except for the occasional passing car, the room was quiet. A gurgle from the faucet seemed unusually loud.

The condition of the rest room made Meat decide that

he didn't have to go after all. He glanced down. The breeze from the window disturbed the paper towels, and Meat saw a wallet. It was light blue.

Meat bent closer. This looked like a guy-ette's wallet. He thought maybe he should check the door again to make sure the sign said Guys—after all, this was a comedy club and people could go in for sick jokes, like Herculeah did. Anyway, he was getting out of here. This place was giving him the creeps.

Meat picked up the wallet and, without opening it, put it in his back pocket. He would turn it in. They probably had some sort of Lost and Found department.

As he turned to go, he noticed a lipstick halfway between where he had found the wallet and the door to one of the stalls. He didn't pick this up. He just stared at it as if trying to make a connection.

The wallet . . .

The lipstick . . .

His eyes continued to look.

A hair brush—a dainty one with speckles like confetti in the plastic.

The objects began to take on the feeling of a trail, things leading to something.

And Meat knew that at the end of the trail there was going to be something he wouldn't like.

Something that would change his life.

And not for the better.

5

THE GUY-ETTE

"Herculeah, come away from the window."

"I have to make sure Meat gets home all right."

"For someone who's not worried about Meat, you are giving a good imitation of being worried about Meat."

"I can't help it."

"What time do you expect him?"

"Nine o'clock." Herculeah glanced over her shoulder at the clock. "Oh, not for another hour."

"Then come away from the window for an hour. Then go back."

Herculeah's mother was at her desk, Herculeah at the living-room window. The living room served as Mim

Jones's office. She was a private investigator and saw her clients here.

"You know, it's funny."

"What? I could use a laugh."

"No, funny odd. Meat has told me that when I'm away and he thinks I'm in trouble, he stands at the window. Now things have turned around. I'm the one standing at the window, and Meat's the one in trouble."

"You don't know that."

Herculeah smoothed down her hair. "I know it," she said.

Meat's eyes continued to focus on the ominous trail. Now he was almost at the door of the stall.

The wallet . . . the lipstick . . . the brush . . . and now—

The purse.

There was the purse, also blue. It lay on its side, with its golden chain broken.

Meat drew in a breath. He paused. Now his mind had begun to reason out what had happened. A guy-ette had mistakenly come into the men's room.

Of course. She had realized her mistake—probably as soon as she saw the urinals—heard him coming and, in a panic, quickly ducked into one of the stalls, hoping not to be discovered. These dropped objects and broken chain were the result of her panic.

Meat was not up on bathroom etiquette, but he knew

that what he needed to do was to leave the room immediately in a gentlemanly way.

He turned, then hesitated. No, maybe he should quickly wash his hands to show he hadn't noticed anything. He did that, running a little cold water on them from the dirty tap. He reached for a towel, but the holder was empty.

He quickly dried his hands on the sides of his pants. He said, "Well, I'd better be getting back to class or they'll start without me." He started for the door.

The wallet! He remembered the wallet. He had the girl's wallet.

And then a sudden thought made his freeze. The lights had been off when he entered. Off!

If there were a girl in here, she would have ducked immediately into one of the stalls, wouldn't she? Particularly if she was in a panic. She wouldn't have wasted time by running across the room and turning off the light first.

Now Meat did not know what to do. He decided the best thing he could do was put the wallet back where he had found it and return to the group.

He reached back to pull the wallet from his pocket, and his elbow hit the door of a stall, jarring it open.

Meat saw a flash of blue. There was someone sitting inside.

He was fairly certain it was a guy-ette.

"Oh, I'm so sorry," Meat said.

He spoke as he would have wanted someone to speak to him in similar circumstances. He knew every restroom nightmare there was, and having a stranger of the opposite sex catch you sitting on the john was right up at the top.

"My elbow did that. My head was turned the other way. I didn't see a thing. Go on with what you were—"

Meat didn't get to say the word "doing," because at that moment something fell against the door of the stall, opening it all the way. Meat stumbled backward.

"I really was looking the other way that time. I didn't even—"

This was another sentence that Meat was not going to complete.

He stepped back quickly. A body had fallen forward from the stall and landed at his feet.

A girl! A girl!

Her head was turned to the side, and a ponytail hid most of her face.

A girl!

And worse than that!

Much, much worse than that.

As bad as it could be.

The girl was dead.

6

STAGE FRIGHT

Meat backed out of the rest room. The door clanged shut behind him, the word "Guys" passed unseen before his fixed gaze. Slowly he began to back his way down the dim hall.

Something seemed to be stuck in his throat. It felt like a rock, but Meat knew it was something worse. Meat knew that it was a scream and that it wouldn't go down, and he hoped it wouldn't come up.

He heard something, a noise that seemed to come from inside the rest room. Footsteps? If Herculeah had been there, she would have rushed forward to investigate, but he was no Herculeah.

He didn't have the strength to move forward and open the door when all he would see would be a dead body. Or maybe he would see something worse. Maybe the footsteps belonged to the killer. Could the killer have been in the bathroom with him and the body? The thought caused him to shudder. Anyway, he told himself, maybe the noise had come from Guy-ettes instead.

He glanced hopefully at that door. He would have given a lot to see it burst open and an armed policewoman step out.

Meat continued his slow backward steps. He heard laughter behind him. He turned, as surprised as if he had never heard the sound before.

Then he realized that the comedy class had started. He continued his long walk, concentrating on putting one foot directly behind the other, on not fainting. He took deep breaths, forgetting that the air was scented with disinfectant and urine.

He paused at the telephone, wanting to call someone, but he couldn't even think of Herculeah's number, the number he had dialed at least three times a day since they had met. He continued with slow heavy steps, helping himself along by touching the wall first on one side and then the other.

The distance from the men's room to the club room where his fellow classmates laughed seemed to be hundreds of miles away, instead of a few feet. He could not remember anything taking him so long.

He came to the end of the hall. Mike had started without him. "Listen, gang, being funny is no joke."

There was laughter.

Mike went on, "The key to being funny is to find out what is interestingly funny about yourself. That's what we're going to start with. What sets you apart. We'll listen to your voice and help you develop your own style. Individuality is the key. The world of comedy rewards originals big-time."

There was a question that Meat couldn't hear.

The teacher said, "I'm going to help you. That's what we're here for. What's funny about you—what works for you."

Meat progressed into the room. He found he was standing on the stage, in what was probably the comedy spotlight. He cleared his throat.

The class looked at him. The teacher turned too, his eyebrows raised in a quizzical way.

There must have been something comical about him— even though he had never felt less funny in his life— because their faces brightened. They were obviously ready to laugh.

Meat swallowed. The sound was loud enough to cause actual smiles.

It was as if they thought he'd gone into the men's room to work up a routine, and now he'd done it. Now he was ready to start his routine, to crack them up. He shook his head.

The teacher encouraged him with a gesture.

"Maybe he's got stage fright," Barbie said, and giggled.

Yes, he had stage fright and every other kind of fright there was in the world.

Meat swallowed. He didn't think he could speak because of the rock in his throat—it might have to be removed surgically.

More smiles, more expectation.

He finally got out the first half of his sentence. "There's a girl in the men's bathroom . . ."

Their faces grew even brighter. Their smiles widened. Meat knew how it would be to be a stand-up comic, to have the entire room waiting for the punch line.

He wished he had a funnier one.

"And she's dead."

7

THE BUSY BODY

"Is that supposed to be funny? Because I don't get it," Barbie said.

A general criticism of his routine began.

"I don't get it either."

"I mean, he started out all right. The part about the girl in the men's room was promising, but a dead body isn't funny at all."

"No, no," Meat shouted over their comments. "I'm not trying to be funny."

He could see that everyone still wanted it to be a joke. Meat did, too.

"Here's what happened." He put up his hands like a traffic cop stopping traffic. "Just listen. Listen!"

The room grew silent.

"I went in the rest room marked Guys, and I turned on the light. And I looked down and saw a wallet and it was light blue. I said to myself, 'Okay, there's a girl's wallet.' I didn't get, like, alarmed, you know."

He made an attempt to swallow, but the scream was still lodged in his throat.

"I glanced toward the stalls and saw a lipstick—a girl's lipstick.

"Then I saw a brush.

"Then I saw a purse.

"Then I saw a foot—a girl's foot."

Meat couldn't remember whether he had actually seen a foot or not, but he could see that he was getting somewhere. He had their serious attention now. A girl's foot couldn't be attached to anything but a girl.

"I was getting ready to leave. I thought, well, a girl has gotten in here by mistake and is too embarrassed to come out . . ."

He made another unsuccessful attempt to swallow.

"I turned to go. And then, and I do not know how this happened, but my elbow hit the door to the stall . . ."

He put one hand to his throat to hold the scream in place. Now was not the time for it to make its appearance.

"And the door opened . . ."

He closed his eyes and attempted to take a deep breath, which couldn't get past the scream.

His voice rose so that his next words were almost a scream. "Andadeadbodyfellout." He tried again. "A dead body fell out."

There was silence. Meat didn't want to, but he knew he had to fill it. "I couldn't see her face because her ponytail, like, fell across it. Anyway, her face was pressed right into the bathroom floor, and nobody but a dead person would press her face against a floor like that."

Mike took two steps forward. "Wait a minute. You're serious, aren't you? You really think you saw a body in the men's room."

"I did see one."

"Okay, okay, sit down. Sit down. Come on over here. Sit down. I'll check it out."

Mike jumped up on the stage and with his hands on Meat's shoulders led him off the stage and back to his table. Meat sank into his chair.

Mike walked quickly to the hallway. "Everybody just stay cool," he advised, and disappeared.

Meat was back at the same table, but it seemed to him that the other two people, Mrs. Santa Claus and Barbie, had shifted their chairs away from him, as if he had something they didn't want to catch.

Under the table his knees had begun to tremble, and Meat was afraid this was just the beginning, that the trembling would move up his body like in the song "Dry Bones."

"You really did see something in there, didn't you?" Mrs. Santa Claus asked finally.

Meat nodded.

"Well, that must have been a terrible shock."

"Yes." Meat gasped out the word. He glanced at the hallway. "I'm wondering if I should call the police. My best friend's dad is a detective with the police department. I could call him. Or nine-one-one! I didn't even think of that. I passed right by the phone."

He made an effort to get to his feet, but his trembling knees wouldn't let him.

"Don't do anything until Mike gets back." Mrs. Santa Claus glanced around. "What's keeping him?"

"When you find a dead body, it takes a lot out of you," Meat said. "I'm speaking from experience."

"Here he comes," someone across the room said.

Mike appeared. He was smiling. "False alarm. There is nobody, dead or otherwise, in the men's room."

Meat stared blankly at Mike.

Mrs. Santa Claus said, "But he really thinks he saw it. And I believe him."

"I don't know what he saw or didn't see."

A man in a backward baseball cap said, "Hey, maybe it's an April Fools' joke. It is April first, you know."

"I think you're right," Mike said quickly. "Yeah, there was a girl in my last class who would do something like this. What color hair did she have?"

"I don't know—brown."

"Yes, that was probably her." Mike came over and put his hand on Meat's shoulder. "I'm just sorry you had to be the victim." He peered closely into Meat's face. "You all right?"

Meat nodded, though he had never been less all right in his life.

Mike turned back to the class. "You've already learned something, see? You've learned something that isn't funny. Now, where was I?"

The man in the backward baseball cap checked his notes. "We have to discover what's interesting and funny about us."

"Yes, you've got to discover your character. Charlie Chaplin had the little tramp. Lily Tomlin had Ernestine; Flip Wilson, Geraldine. So that's your goal. To discover your character. You go onstage and you are the character.

"Now who wants to go first?"

Meat raised his hand.

"Great, Meat, I'm glad to see you've snapped back. Come on up here."

"No, I wasn't raising my hand for that. I just feel like maybe I want to go home."

"Now, boys and girls . . ." This was Mush Mouth talking, but he grinned and went on in his own voice. "Of course you want to go home. We spend our whole lives wanting to go home. Our mothers program that into us. Even when we are home, we want to go home. We must fight the urge to go home. Will you please stay—just to prove that I am stronger than your mom?"

Meat nodded.

"Now, who's first?"

The man with the backward baseball cap got up, but Mrs. Santa Claus beat him out.

"Well, maybe this isn't so funny," she said, "but everybody is always telling me I look like Mrs. Santa Claus."

"I like it. I like it," Mike said.

"So anyway. It's hard living with elves . . ."

Meat's mind was not on elves. He couldn't even remember if there really was a Mrs. Santa Claus.

Meat's mind was on murder.

8

THE OLYMPIC SCREAM

Meat stepped outside Funny Bonz and took a deep breath of cool night air. He needed it.

It was nine o'clock. Meat had somehow managed to get through the two hours of comedy class, but he had not learned one thing about begin funny.

The rest of the class obviously had. They had stayed behind to chat. As Meat left the room, the man in the backward baseball cap was flapping his arms. "Do I look enough like a goose when I do this?" Next to him, Barbie was telling someone, "I wish I could find some Barbie jokes. I mean, there have to be a zillion of them—and Ken—he's such a nerd."

It didn't surprise Meat that no one had urged him to

stay. Not that he would have. Nothing—no one—could have held him there.

"Don't forget your assignment," Mike called to Meat as he reached the door. Meat waved without looking around. He didn't know what the assignment was. He didn't care. He was never coming back.

Meat turned to the left and began walking home. He knew every store and building on this street, but tonight it was a street where the trees threw dead men's shadows on the white concrete, and no cars passed. No people either.

Where was everybody? Meat had undergone such an ordeal that maybe the rest of the world had, too. Maybe he and the stupid people at Funny Bonz were all that was left.

Meat paused at the curb. Then the thought that he had been holding off all through the miserable evening rose before him like an atomic cloud—and, to him, just as threatening.

He had seen a dead girl. He had. This was an indisputable fact.

And, he went on to himself, there's a big difference between a dead girl and somebody playing an April Fool joke.

No living person would press her face against that restroom floor with the dirty paper towels and roaches and . . . whatever. The very thought made him sick.

And nobody could hold still like that for that long.

Without even being aware of what he was doing, he

crossed the street, arguing with himself the way he would like to have argued with those stupid people at Funny Bonz, especially Mike.

And, speaking of Mike, why had he stayed so long when he went to check the rest room? It would only take a minute to open the door and see that there was no dead body, wouldn't it? He wouldn't even have to click on the light.

And even if he had decided to check both bathrooms—just to be on the safe side—even if he had decided to *use* both bathrooms, it still wouldn't have taken that long.

The four blocks to Meat's house, which he had covered with such speed and hope two hours before, now seemed endless. He paused to check his surroundings, thinking perhaps he had missed his turn. He hadn't.

What if Mike had moved the body? That would account for the time he'd been gone. But why would he do that? That would be a crime. There was a name for it. What was it? What was it?

Meat said the words, "Accessory to murder," but instead of feeling a sense of satisfaction at coming up with the right phrase, a sense of foreboding came over him, a chill on the back of his neck.

Someone was behind him.

He dared not look around. He couldn't hear anything, but that meant nothing. He seemed to be in a pocket of silence. He began to walk faster.

Now he heard it. A footstep.

He broke into a run. Now the footsteps were running

too, closing the distance. Whoever it was was sure to catch him. He was the slowest runner he knew. And tonight he seemed to be running in molasses, his feet sticking to the pavement.

His street was just ahead. If he could reach that . . . turn the corner . . .

A terrible thought turned his blood to ice. He was the only person—other than the murderer—who had seen the body. And if the murderer caught him, killed him—and that's what killers did—then there would be nobody who had seen it.

As he rounded his corner, the thing that he had feared the most in the world happened. Fingers grabbed him by the arm.

He gave one desperate twist to free himself, but the fingers held, drew him into the shadows.

Meat opened his mouth.

And the scream that had been stuck in his throat all evening, the scream that he had thought would have to be surgically removed, came loose, flooding his mouth.

It burst from him, and it was a scream that went through every door, every window on the block.

It was a scream to be proud of, even if it was probably the last sound he would ever make.

If screaming were an Olympic event, Meat would have gotten a ten.

9

PROOF POSITIVE

"Do you need help?"

"Is anything wrong out there?"

"Want me to call the police?"

Before Meat could scream, "YES!" to all three questions someone behind him called, "No, no. It's just us—Herculeah Jones and Meat."

It was Herculeah's voice. Meat turned. He looked around in astonishment. It was Herculeah holding his arm. Herculeah!

"You're sure you're both all right?"

"Yes. Yes, we're fine!"

The doors closed. The dogs were hushed. The street grew silent again.

When Herculeah spoke, her voice had lost its cheerful, everything's-all-right, go-back-to-what-you-were-doing tone.

"What has happened, Meat?" she asked in a low voice.

Meat still didn't speak.

"You're shaking. What's going on?"

When Meat finally spoke, it was an accusation. "Why didn't you let me know it was you back there? Why didn't you call my name?"

"I did. I've been calling your name for two blocks!"

"Then why didn't I hear you?"

"I don't know. I finished taking my last pictures and decided to drop the film off at the camera shop, and Funny Bonz was on the way home, sort of, so I stopped in. They said you'd left, and I finally saw you and you walked like this and stopped like this and did that . . ."

She paused to imitate his movement.

He was always offended by Herculeah's imitations. He said coldly, "Well, if you had just come across a dead body, perhaps you would be doing this and that, too."

"A dead body!"

"Yes."

"A dead body! Meat, for once in your life, be original."

He fell back as if he had been struck a direct blow, which he had.

"I pulled that this afternoon," Herculeah went on. "I found a dead body, remember? A squirrel. April Fool!"

"This was no squirrel, and I'm not the sadistic sort of person who does April Fool jokes. I am thankful to say

I'm beyond that. When I say I found a dead body, I found a dead body!"

He turned and walked away. Herculeah watched for a moment and then followed.

"So where was the dead body?" she asked.

"What do you care?"

"I care. Where was it?"

"In the bathroom."

She couldn't help herself. She snickered. Meat thought she would have been one of those fourth-graders who loved Mike's imitation of Mush Mouth.

"Never mind," he said coldly.

"Oh, come on. Where was it?"

"In the bathroom!" He spoke these three words through his teeth to give them extra force. He could see the spit in the light from the streetlight.

"I went into the bathroom at Funny Bonz—the men's room. Guys. I could tell it from the girls' bathroom because that was Guy-ettes. I walked in. The light was out. I turned it on. There was a wallet on the floor. There was a lipstick beyond it, closer to a stall. Then there was a brush, then a purse. Then the stall door came open and there was a body!"

The way he said it left Herculeah with no doubt that he had lived it.

"Whose body was it?"

"A girl. That's all I know. I couldn't see her face—her ponytail fell forward and hid it."

"Like Madame Rosa," Herculeah said. "Remember

when I found Madame Rosa's body, her hair was across her face? If I had lifted her hair and checked, then I would never have gotten in so much trouble."

Meat wanted to say, "This is my murder, if you don't mind, not yours," but before he could do that, Herculeah spoke again.

"Go on."

"I came out. I told everybody I'd found a body. Mike— that's the teacher—said he'd check it out. In about a hundred hours he came back and said it was a false alarm. 'No body, living or dead, in the rest rooms, so let's get on with the class.'"

"And then?"

"Then we got on with the class."

"Did he give any explanation."

"He claimed he had a student who liked to play practical jokes. There are people like that."

Herculeah recognized this as an insult, but she didn't take offense.

"Maybe it was."

He shook his head. "I forgot one very important thing. The rest room floor was so gross I didn't even want to walk on it. You'd have to be dead to press your face against it."

"You're probably right."

"In the middle of the class a guy wearing a backward baseball cap went to the rest room and when he came back, I looked at him, like I wanted to know if he'd seen a body, and he shook his head."

"Could you have imagined it, Meat?"

"No! No! You're just like everybody else. You . . ."

He stopped. He took in a breath. He put one hand to his back pocket.

"I didn't imagine it. I can prove it."

"How?"

"I just remembered something."

"What?"

"I picked up something off the floor."

"What?"

Meat reached into his back pocket.

"This," he said.

In his hand was a blue wallet.

10

NAME OF THE GAME

"Open it, open it!" Herculeah said.

"I will. Give me a chance."

Meat opened the wallet and peered inside.

"Get under the streetlight!"

Herculeah pushed him closer to the streetlight and peered over his shoulder.

"Can you make out the name?"

"Marcie . . . Marcie Mullet." Meat gave the words a ghostly reading. "Marcie Mullet." Then he added, "Oh!" as if he had been stung.

"What?"

"One of the students didn't show up."

"If she was dead, she couldn't."

"I'm trying to remember what he said—just that it was a very funny person." Meat shuddered.

"Address?" Herculeah asked briskly, getting back to business.

"Thirteen twenty-nine Broadview."

"Broadview! Meat, you know where that is, don't you? It's just two streets over. Come on."

"Where?"

"To Broadview! To Marcie Mullet's!"

"I don't think that's such a good idea."

"Why?"

"I just don't think I could stand to see a dead body one more time tonight."

"But, don't you get it? We go there to return the wallet. We knock at the door and ask for Marcie Mullet. If she comes to the door, she's not dead. If she doesn't come to the door . . . well, we'll worry about that when it happens. Come on."

Meat followed Herculeah, but with such lack of enthusiasm that she had to turn around twice to say, "Come on. Listen, Meat, I've got to get home. My mother only let me go out to turn in the film, because I kept bugging her. Then I had to promise I'd go straight there."

"You broke your promise."

"I did not. I went straight there. It's on the way home that I'm going a few blocks out of the way."

As they turned onto Broadview, Herculeah began calling out the numbers. "Eleven-thirty . . ."

"Is it that late?" Meat asked, alarmed.

"No, that's the number of the house. It's going to be on the other side of the street—two blocks down."

"Eleven . . . twelve . . . thirteen—this is the right block."

Herculeah began walking even faster. She was so far ahead of Meat now that he just stopped and watched tiredly. He leaned against a lamppost for support.

Broadview didn't live up to its name. The houses were close together; the street, narrow. The houses went up two and three stories with attics above, but now there were extra mailboxes on the porches to show multiple occupancy.

Herculeah danced her way down the block. Suddenly she stopped and turned to beckon to him. Meat walked slowly forward and stopped beside her. They looked up at the house together.

There were eight mailboxes on this porch, so the house must have been divided into eight small apartments.

"Come on," she said.

She went up the stairs and peered at the nameplates on the mailboxes. "Marcie Mullet," Herculeah read. "She's number seven." Herculeah flipped up the lid of the mailbox. "No mail."

She tried the front door. When it opened, she turned her delighted face to Meat and signaled him to come on. He followed her into a small, dingy lobby. Perhaps it had once been the front parlor of the house. There were eight plastic buttons on the wall beside a desk. Herculeah punched number seven.

They could hear a buzzer sound upstairs, but nobody came down.

"Let's go," Meat said impatiently.

A man unfolded himself from a lean-back chair and peered at them. "Who're you looking for?"

Meat gasped with fright, but Herculeah, again, seemed pleased.

"We're looking for Marcie Mullet," Herculeah told him. "Apartment seven. We've got something of hers we need to return."

"Not in," he answered.

"What time does she usually get in?"

"No telling."

"Do you happen to know where she went tonight?"

The man thought about it. "Seems like she said she was going to some restaurant. What was the name of it? It'll come to me."

Herculeah couldn't wait for him to remember. "Funny Bonz?"

Meat's heart was in his throat as he waited for the answer.

The man smiled. "That's it. Funny Bonz."

Herculeah and Meat looked at each other. Neither had anything to say.

"If you want to leave something for Miss Mullet, I'll see she get's it."

"No," Herculeah said. "We need to see her. It's sort of important."

When they were on the street again, heading for

home, Herculeah added, "It's real important. In the morning first thing, we'll come back to Broadview and—" She broke off. "No, first thing I'm going to pick up my photos. Meat, for some reason, those nineteen exposures are almost as much a mystery to me as Marcie Mullet. Anyway, after I see my photos, we're off to Broadview."

Meat said, "In the morning, first thing, we ought to call your dad."

"And tell him what? That you thought you saw a dead body? On April Fool's Day?" She sighed with frustration. "If we had the body, I would already have called."

"We have the wallet."

"But what does that prove?"

Meat was silent.

"You know how my dad feels about my playing detective."

"But that's what you are doing."

"Well, I'll think about it. Maybe I'll call him, maybe I won't. Satisfied?"

Meat was not satisfied at all, but he nodded.

"I'll see you in the morning."

"Right."

It was a morning Meat did not look forward to. But then, he told himself, remembering the events of the evening, mornings are usually better than nights.

A small voice reminded him, Not always.

11

NINETEEN EXPOSURES

"Herculeah!"

Herculeah came around the corner fast, just as she had yesterday. Meat thought at first she was hurrying toward him—perhaps to show him her photos—but she did not glance across the street. That was strange. She had to have heard him.

Meat moved to the steps of the porch and started down.

"Herculeah!"

Again she did not glance in his direction. What was going on? Was she getting ready to pull another of those stupid jokes?

He crossed the street, moving with a speed that surprised him. It surprised Herculeah too, from the look on her face when she saw him blocking the steps to her house.

"Herculeah—"

She looked at him as if she did not know him. Her expression was one he had not seen before—strange and unreadable.

"What's wrong?"

Her stare was blank. It was as if she had had a shock so devastating that she couldn't take in anything normal.

"Did you get your photos? I'm sorry I didn't act particularly interested and—okay, I'm sorry I got mad yesterday over your taking my picture—but what with finding the dead body and all . . ."

He glanced down. In her hand was a yellow and black envelope from Cameras, Inc.

"Oh, you got them. I'd like to see them." He didn't really want to, but being a good sport, he held out his hand.

Herculeah clutched the envelope against her as if protecting it.

"They can't have been that bad," he said. "Well, the ones of me could have." His hand was still extended. Herculeah looked down at it as if it were the hand from a horror movie.

"Is there something wrong with the pictures?"

She didn't answer.

"Or is it that you went to Broadview. Is that it? Did you

see Marcie Mullet? Is she dead? Is that what's wrong?"

She shook her head, and Meat realized that what was wrong had nothing to do with the body at Funny Bonz but with the pictures in Herculeah's hand.

"You might as well let me see them."

No reaction.

"You know you'll show them to me sooner or later."

Now she spoke for the first time. One word. "Maybe."

"So why not now?"

She clutched the photos tighter against her.

"Later? What time? Today? Tomorrow?"

"I don't know. I can't think. I just don't know."

With that, she swirled past him and fumbled with her key as she tried to unlock her door.

"Aren't we going to Broadview?"

He had never seen Herculeah have trouble unlocking a door before. He had even seen her break locks.

"I thought we were going to Broadview. Remember Marcie Mullet? Remember Funny Bonz?"

She redoubled her efforts on the lock. It gave. The door opened, and in one swift movement Herculeah was inside.

Meat went quickly up the steps and glanced in the small window beside the door. All he could see was the back of Herculeah's coat. It was as if getting in the door was so stressful that Herculeah had to lean against the first thing she came to for support.

He rapped on the glass. "Are you all right?"

No answer.

"Is it something about the pictures?"

No answer.

"Is it something about me? Something I did?"

No answer.

"Well, at least let me in. I hate it when people won't let me in. I won't mention the photos and I won't mention Marcie Mullet. Just let me in."

Herculeah shook her head in a movement that was almost desperate. He watched as she ran up the stairs to her room and disappeared from view.

Meat continued to peer through the dusty glass. Something was terribly wrong. Was it something about the pictures? Something about the murder?

He couldn't stand it. He rang the doorbell. Even as he pressed the bell and heard the ding-dong, he felt this was stupid and useless. When minutes passed and Herculeah did not come to the door, he knew it.

Still, he couldn't help trying one more time.

Ding-dong.

There ought to be at least two different rings for a doorbell, he thought, ding-dong when you were stopping by for a friendly chat and . . . He couldn't think of any sound that would show the depth of his need right now.

Slowly, shoulders sagging, Meat headed for home. He took his place in the living room, at the window, watching the house in case she reappeared.

But hours passed, and she did not.

———

Inside her bedroom, Herculeah sat on the side of her bed, still in her coat, clutching the envelope containing the photographs against her chest.

She had been so excited about getting the pictures, she had arrived even before the camera shop was open. It was a strange excitement, not entirely pleasant.

At last Cameras, Inc., opened the door and the envelope was in her hand. She had opened it there at the counter, tearing the flap of the envelope in her haste.

"Some of the older photos are kind of dark," the clerk told her. "I tried to lighten them, but sometimes when the film's been in the camera awhile . . ."

The recent photos came first, one of her mom in the kitchen, one of her. Herculean smiled at the two of Meat.

Then came the pictures that had been taken long ago, the dark ones. The smile faded from Herculeah's face.

She had moved to the front of the store and the light from the window. She couldn't believe what she was seeing.

"Is there anything wrong?" the clerk called from the counter. "I could probably lighten them a bit if I had more time. You wanted them this morning," he reminded her.

Herculeah didn't answer. She crammed the pictures back into the envelope and ran out the door. Clutching them against her, she had run for home.

The last person in the world she had wanted to see was

Meat. She knew she was hurting him by not answering his questions. But showing him the photographs would have hurt him much more.

Behind her, Tarot the parrot said, "Beware! Beware!" Herculeah did not even hear him. "Oh, Mom!" he said in Herculeah's own voice. He had picked this up without any help.

Herculeah didn't react.

Since Tarot's entire vocabulary consisted of these few words, he closed his eyes and went back to sleep.

On the bed Herculeah sat without moving, waiting for her mother to come home and tell her what to do.

Hurry, Mom, Herculeah thought. Hurry!

12

MEAT ON HIS OWN

Meat sat in front of the telephone. He was trying not to call Herculeah. He began doodling on the telephone pad.

He remembered that when he was three he would write like this, big loopy letters, and when he had a page full he would run to his dad. "Another story?" his dad would say. "Want me to read it to you?"

Meat's happiest memories of his dad were sitting on his lap, listening to the funny stories Meat had written.

"Hey, this is about a Flapdoodle. I didn't know you knew what a Flapdoodle was!"

Meat was surprised to find that in the middle of this pleasant memory, he had dialed Herculeah's phone number. Well, he had tried.

On the third ring a recorded voice came on. These recorded voices were always so cheerful, Meat thought, making callers who weren't cheerful feel even worse. Mrs. Jones said, "This is Mim Jones. I can't take your call right now, but you can leave a message at the beep, and I'll get back to you."

At the beep, Meat cleared his throat and said, "Herculeah, I'm going back to Broadview to look for Marcie Mullet. If you don't want to come with me, fine! I'll go alone. Good-bye."

He hung up the phone, proud that he had resisted the urge to revert to childishly adding fourteen or fifteen *please*s.

He took a deep breath. Now that he had announced his intention, he had to carry it out. He had to go to Broadview.

Meat put on his jacket and went out onto the front porch. He took more time than necessary zipping his jacket up. He kept his eyes on the upstairs window of Herculeah's bedroom. He knew that was where she was and maybe if she saw him . . .

To give her plenty of time, he took out the blue wallet and opened it. He stared at Marcie Mullet's ID picture on her driver's license. The picture didn't actually look like the girl on the bathroom floor. Her hair had been straighter and longer, but sometimes girls changed things like that.

The statistics didn't quite fit, either—five feet seven inches tall, 185 pounds. The girl on the bathroom floor had seemed taller than that, thinner too. Of course he wasn't an expert on girls' sizes.

He checked the rest of the wallet, though he knew the contents—no folding money, three quarters, two dimes.

But wait. What was this? There was a folded piece of paper behind the driver's license.

Meat took it out and unfolded it. He read the words and drew in his breath.

"All right. All right. I'll be at F.B. at 7:00. We'll talk."

F.B. Funny Bonz.

And seven o'clock was about the time he found the body.

He glanced again at Herculeah's bedroom window. He wanted to run across the street, beat on the door.

"I found a note—a note. You have to see this!" he wanted to read it aloud, giving it the menacing quality he felt it deserved.

But he had been left standing at Herculeah's front door enough times today. He went down the steps and at the corner turned toward Broadview.

Herculeah watched from her mother's office window as he put on his jacket and went through the blue wallet.

She watched intently as he discovered the piece of paper, watched as he unfolded it. The look on his face made her want to run across the street and read the message for herself. But she couldn't face Meat, not yet.

When Meat was out of sight, Herculeah picked up the phone and dialed a number of her own.

"Police Department, zone three. This is Captain Morrison. Can I help you?"

"Hi, it's Herculeah Jones, Captain. I want to speak to my dad."

"He's not here, but I can give him a call if it's important."

"I'm afraid it is."

Herculeah waited until he came back on the line.

"Did you get him?" she asked.

"Yes, he's out that way. He says he'll stop by on his way back to the station."

"Oh, thanks."

She hung up the phone and waited, walking back and forth in front of the window until she saw her father's car. She burst through the front door and was on the sidewalk before her father had opened the door.

"Hi, Dad, I am so glad to see you. Can you come inside? Please!"

"I've got a few minutes. What's up?"

"Two things really," she said as they went up the steps. "One is sort of, well, police business."

"Oh?"

"I was wondering—well, Met thought he found a dead body last night."

"Herculeah, you kids have got to stop finding dead bodies—"

"Just listen, Dad, please. Don't give me the finding-dead-bodies lecture. Meat went into the bathroom of Funny Bonz. Funny Bonz is a comedy club in the basement of the old hotel. There was a body on the floor—it sort of fell out of the toilet stall. Well, then the man who runs the club, Mike Howard—"

"Mike Howard . . . Mike Howard," her father said as if he were turning through a mental Rolodex.

"Yes, Mike Howard. And this is really suspicious. Mike Howard goes to check and he is gone a long time—much longer than it would take him to check. And then he comes back and says there was no body—that it was probably some sort of April Fools' joke."

"Maybe it was. And it's not unusual for people to do drugs in public rest rooms."

"I guess, but I was wondering if a body fitting this description had turned up. The corpse was a girl with brown hair, maybe dyed. Her name could be Marcie Mullet."

"Is Meat at home?" her father interrupted.

"No."

"I'd like to hear what he's got to say about this."

"He could have gone over to Marcie Mullet's house—it's on Broadview—thirteen twenty-nine."

How do you know the name and address of this dead body?"

"I don't. I'm just telling you what Meat told me."

"I'll swing by there."

"And, Dad, about the dead bodies?"

"I am happy to say we have no dead bodies, identified or not."

"You probably wouldn't tell me if you did."

There was a silence. Then her father said, "So what else is bothering you?"

"Dad, this is one of the worst things that has ever happened to me in my life."

"Not again."

"I'm serious this time. I bought a camera in Hidden Treasures yesterday. I don't know why I bought it except that I was drawn to it."

"Why can't you shop at the mall like other girls?"

"Oh, Dad. But even as I was buying it, something was bothering me about the other objects for sale on the table. Like I'd seen them before."

"So?"

"But I couldn't think where. Anyway, whoever had owned the camera had taken nineteen exposures. I finished the roll and got it developed." She paused to swallow. "Well, there were five pictures of Meat and Mom that I took and nineteen others."

"So?"

"The other pictures were taken a long time ago— maybe ten years ago."

"So?"

"And I know the people in the pictures."

"Herculeah, don't make me keep saying, 'So.' Just tell me what's upset you about these pictures."

"They're of Meat."

"Meat across the street?"

"Yes, Meat and his dad. Well, seven of them are of

Meat and his father doing normal things—like standing in front of the house and sitting on the front steps. There's one of them in the park, and one Meat must have taken of his dad because his head's cut off. Those were normal, everyday pictures like any father and son would take.

"And then I remembered where I'd seen all those other things at Hidden Treasures before. One time I was over at Meat's and he went into his mother's room. He'd bought some pecan rolls from the Lion's Club and they'd disappeared, and Meat suspected she'd hidden them in her closet.

"So I stood outside the door as a lookout to warn Meat if his mom came home. Finally, I got curious about what was taking him so long and I went in there and he had a whole box of stuff—and now I remember that most of what was in that box was on the same table with the camera. Meat's mom must have cleaned out her closet and taken all the stuff to Hidden Treasures." She looked at her dad.

"And then, wouldn't you know it, Mrs. Mac came in and caught us. Meat blurted out that he was looking for his pecan rolls, he knew she'd hidden them, and she said that she'd found the empty wrappers when she was making up his bed that morning, that he must have eaten them in his sleep."

"The pictures?" her father said tiredly.

"Oh, yes, sorry. I got carried away."

She handed him the seven pictures, and he shuffled through them, glancing at each one for only a moment. He looked up at her. "I take it there's more."

"Yes, the rest are of his father dressed for—" She made a face. "For, I guess you'd say, work."

"What kind of work did he do?"

With a sigh she handed her father the rest of the photographs.

"See for yourself," she said.

13

BAD NEWS

Meat approached 1329 Broadview with caution. He was on the opposite side of the street and he paused periodically to tie and retie his shoelaces. He had seen spies do this to make sure they weren't being followed. As he worked on his shoelaces he glanced up and down the street.

He straightened once again and went over his plans. He would cross the street, go up to the house, enter, and ring Marcie Mullet's bell. If she answered, he would ask to speak to her. "I have something that belongs to you," he said, speaking out loud. He put one hand over his back pocket to make sure the wallet was still there.

A car pulled up beside him and a voice said, "Just the man I was looking for."

Meat stared. He hadn't heard or seen the car approaching. Although Meat didn't think he was either a man or someone being looked for, he glanced around.

It was Chico Jones, Herculeah's dad, and Meat was very glad to see him.

"Mr. Jones, what are you doing here?"

"I stopped by the house, and Herculeah told me you might be here." Chico Jones got out of the car and put one hand on Meat's shoulder. Meat couldn't remember him doing that before. Maybe Chico Jones suspected him of something.

"You talked to Herculeah?" he asked.

"She told me about what happened last night at Funny Bonz. I thought I'd check and make sure this—" he paused to look at his notes—"Marcie Mullet's all right."

"Can I go with you? I want to know if she's all right, too." It was extremely pleasant to have Chico Jones on his side.

"You wait in the car. I want to talk to you."

"But—"

He held the car door open like a policeman and Meat got in like a victim. He watched as Chico Jones went up the walkway to 1329.

Even though Meat was extremely glad to have run into Chico Jones, he was uneasy about the way Chico Jones was treating him. Herculeah's dad was being too nice. Also, his look seemed more piercing than usual, as if he were actually trying to see into his brain—the way Herculeah frequently did.

He glanced out the window. Beside him the police radio sputtered with requests and information.

Could Herculeah have said something to her dad—something about—he couldn't think of anything to explain Herculeah's behavior. It was almost scary the way she was avoiding him, as if he had some terrible illness.

Suddenly, Chico Jones was coming down the steps, down the sidewalk.

"Not there," Chico Jones said.

"And nobody's seen her?"

"No, but the superintendent heard someone in the apartment during the night." Chico Jones turned his head to Meat. "So. What happened last night?"

"I was at Funny Bonz—that's a comedy club—and I went to the bathroom."

"What time?"

"A little after seven. And there was a dead body in one of the stalls. It fell forward into the room."

"You're sure the person was dead?"

"She wasn't moving."

"Did you feel for a pulse?"

"No, I couldn't."

"See any blood?"

"No."

"And what? You went back to the room where the class was being held?"

Meat felt that Chico Jones wasn't asking his usual

sharp questions. It was as if something had distracted him.

"Yes, and I told Mike—"

"Mike Howard." Another turn through the mental Rolodex.

"Yes, Mike Howard. I told him I'd found a dead body and he went and checked it out and came back and said there wasn't anyone there. He claimed it was an April Fools' joke. Another person went to the rest room later and didn't see anything either."

"Well, I'll check it out, Meat."

"Will you let me know what you find? Herculeah probably won't tell me anything. She's avoiding me these days."

He watched Chico Jones closely to see his reaction. Chico Jones gave him another of those sympathetic looks that Meat didn't care for.

"You'll be the first to know," he said cheerfully.

Meat got out of the car. He waited for Chico to start the motor, but he didn't. He leaned out and said, "Go on home, Meat. Herculeah's got something she wants to talk to you about."

"What?"

"I'll let her do the honors."

And Chico Jones drove away.

He knows what it is, Meat thought, and it's bad news. It's such bad news that he couldn't even tell me, and that's part of a policeman's training—to tell people bad news.

Everybody knows what the bad news is but me.

14

UNLUCKY SEVEN

When Chico Jones's police car had rounded the corner and was out of sight, Meat sighed. Well, there was nothing to do now but go home and hear the bad news.

He looked up at the house, and his hand covered his back pocket. The wallet. He should have given it to Chico Jones. It was the only real evidence he had. But somehow he wasn't ready to give it up. It was his excuse for asking questions, for solving the mystery.

As Meat watched, a face appeared in one of the upstairs windows. The face disappeared at once, as if someone had ducked out of sight.

Marcie Mullet? Meat thought. Could she have hidden from Chico Jones? That was everyone's first instinct—to hide from a policeman. Well, she might not hide from him, Meat. After all, he had something that belonged to her.

He went quickly up the walkway to the house. He opened the front door, which wasn't locked, and peered into the lobby. No one was there.

Slowly he mounted the stairs, taking them one by one. He felt as if he were doing something illegal, but, he told himself, he was just going up to see if Marcie Mullet was home because, see, he had her wallet and wanted to return it.

The door to apartment seven was open. Meat stuck his head inside.

"Marcie?" he called. "Miss Mullet?" That was better.

The man he and Herculeah had met last night said, "She's gone. A policeman was just here and I opened the door for him. I have a key. And look at the place."

The room was a mess—clothes everywhere. Meat took in the display in silence. He was genuinely shocked, not just at the tumble of clothing but at the size of the garments. There were bras capable of holding two melons, and skirts like collapsed tents. He forced himself to look away and up at the man.

"Did she always keep her room like this?" Meat asked.

"I wouldn't know. This is the first time I've been inside."

"But you know her?"

"Yes."

"Can I ask you something?"

"What?"

"Was she—" he glanced at the bra—"was she a . . . large girl?"

"Oh, yeah."

He glanced around the room again. "Maybe somebody broke in and was looking for something and tore the place up."

"It's possible."

"Well, if you see her—"

"That's not likely."

"I know, but if you do, tell her I've got her wallet."

"What's your name?"

"Meat McMannis."

The man pulled the door to, locked it, and paused. "I heard somebody in here last night—late. It didn't sound like her—lots of fast movement. I thought maybe it was that boyfriend of hers—the funny one."

"Funny how?" Meat asked. "I mean, funny ha-ha or funny weird?"

The man gave it some thought.

"Both," he said.

After that, Meat went back down the steps and out into the sunlight. He didn't want to go home, because there wasn't anything to do there but hear the bad news from Herculeah.

He decided to walk past Funny Bonz. He wouldn't go inside—just stroll past.

To reinforce the decision, he said to himself, "I will not

go inside. No matter how tempted I am, I will not go inside."

The first time he passed the building, he gave it a glancing look. It appeared empty. He walked to the corner and crossed the street. This time he paused to put his foot on a fire hydrant, check his shoelaces, and take a better look.

No lights were on. Nobody was there.

"It wouldn't hurt," he said to himself, "to just see if the alley door is locked."

He crossed the street and went up the darkened alley. There was something about the alley that filled him with dread. "If I were Herculeah, my hair would be frizzling."

He paused at the door. "I will not go inside. No matter how tempted I am, I will not go inside."

As he spoke sternly to himself, his hand, moving as if on its own, reached out and turned the doorknob.

15

THE MESSAGE

For the past hour Herculeah had been steeling herself to face Meat and show him the pictures. It helped her to remember what her father had said.

"You have to show him the pictures, hon. You don't have any choice."

"But, Dad, he thinks of his father as this tremendous person."

"Well," her father nodded at the pictures in Herculeah's hands, "he's tremendous, all right."

"Oh, Dad, don't try to be funny. Help me."

"Herculeah, you've always told me that the most important thing to Meat was knowing who his father is."

"But—"

"You told me he went to Madame Rosa to have her try and find him."

"All Madame Rosa told him was she saw shoes."

Again he indicated the snapshots. "There you go."

Herculeah looked down at the shoes in the pictures and grimaced.

"And he went to have his dad's handwriting analyzed. Herculeah, your best friend is frantic for word of his father, and you have not got the right to keep it from him."

She went through the pictures one more time, then put them facedown on the table. She started for the front door.

The message light on the answering machine was blinking. Herculeah crossed the room and punched Play, even though she might have been stalling for time.

The message was from Meat.

"Herculeah, I'm going back to Broadview to look for Marcie Mullet. If you don't want to come with me, fine! I'll go alone. Good-bye."

He had to be back by now, she thought. Squaring her shoulders, she crossed the street and rang the bell.

Mrs. McMannis opened the door. "Can Meat come over to my house?" Herculeah asked. "I've got something to show him."

"Meat's not here."

"Oh."

"He went out a little while ago and hasn't come back. What's going on?"

"I don't know."

Mrs. McMannis gave her a suspicious look. "I think you do."

Herculeah shrugged. She could feel Mrs. Mac's sharp eyes watching her as she crossed the street. At the steps to her house, Herculeah paused.

Meat might be at Marcie Mullet's apartment right now, she thought. What if my dad got an urgent call and Meat's there alone? What if the murderer's there? Meat could be in real trouble.

She thought of the photos inside.

"Double trouble," she said.

16

A BODY IN THE CLOSET

Herculeah tried the front door of Funny Bonz. It was locked.

She knew Meat was inside.

She knocked at the door. "Meat?"

No answer.

The man at the apartment had told her that Meat had left there over a half hour ago. He had not gone home, so he must have come here.

And, Herculeah reminded himself, Meat was not the kind of person who could take care of himself in a scary situation, not the way she could.

She peered through the glass beside the door. She

could see nothing. She thought she heard voices. She knocked again. "Is anybody there?"

No answer.

She remembered a side entrance—Meat had said something about a door on the alley.

Moving quickly, she skirted the building and turned into the alley. The walls of the buildings on either side were so covered with spray paint and graffiti that they were a tangle of letters. Only an occasional word leaped out at her—"Spider" . . . "Zippo" . . . "Beware of" . . .

The Dumpster at the end of the alley had been spray-painted too, so that it blended into the background, almost camouflaged.

Her steps slowed as she approached the door. Her hair had begun to frizzle.

She turned the doorknob. The door opened quietly—she had almost expected it to creak. Taking a deep breath, she stepped inside.

Herculeah moved silently up the few steps and stood in the hall. Suddenly she heard voices to the left.

Herculeah glanced around. Her hair had doubled in size now and she knew she didn't want to be found here in this dark hall.

She glanced over her shoulder and saw a door. JANITOR, the sign said. Herculeah opened it and slipped inside.

It was a closet of cleaning supplies. Herculeah stood there, scarcely breathing, and when she did, she almost choked on the menthol smell of urinal cakes and damp dry-mops and kerosene rags.

Now the voices were closer. Two people were coming down the hall. Men.

Herculeah could make out what they were saying.

"You mean the body's still here? You didn't get rid of it?"

"I thought it was gone. Man, you have a dead body on your hands and then it's gone, you don't go looking for it. I thought I was in the clear."

"If I'm gonna help, I gotta know what's going on."

"Right. Last night some kid goes to the john and comes back. This is a funny kid, but not intentionally. He walks out on the stage. His face was like this."

Herculeah knew he was probably twisting his face, Jim Carrey–like, into Meat's. The other man gave a short, reluctant laugh, as if he couldn't help himself.

"The kid goes, 'There's a girl in the men's bathroom.'"

The voice was so like Meat's that Herculeah was glad he wasn't here to hear it.

"The class starts grinning. They, me, everybody, we think he's doing a routine. Then he goes, 'And she's dead.' Everybody's looking at everybody else to see if they got it. They think they've missed something.

"Anyway, I go back, check the rest room out and, man, there really is a body. It's a kid was in my class last time, back for more—thinks he's ready for the big time."

"And?"

"And, okay, I panicked, there's no other word for it, and my adrenaline was pumping so fast. I got that body out of there and into the closet in minutes. Okay, I should have called the police, but the last thing I need right now is a dead body in the bathroom. I got enough dead bodies sitting in the audience every night. And this club has got to work. I owe money to people you do not want to owe money to—so I got the body out of there."

"And?"

"And I hid it."

Herculeah swallowed. The men's voices were just outside the janitor's door now.

"Where?"

"The first place I could find."

There was a silence, and in that awful moment, Herculeah imagined the men's faces turning to the janitor's closet. Her blood froze. They were going to open the door and find not a dead body but her.

Then the realization hit with the force of a hammer. They would find her *and* the body. The body was here. In the closet with her.

It had to be on the floor behind her. Not again! she thought with growing horror. The body she'd found at Dead Oaks had left her with a dread of it ever happening again. She began to tremble.

She remembered now that in that brief moment before she closed the closet door, she had been aware of something. It hadn't registered then—perhaps it had been some clothes on a coatrack or some old cleaning rags. She hadn't paid much attention.

She should have.

A Herculeah Jones Mystery

Now she knew the truth. There was a dead body in those clothes.

She felt a scream building within her.

Yes, she thought. Yes! She would scream, burst open the door, dash past the startled men, and be outside before they could stop her.

Before she could put the plan into effect, a hand from the back of the closet reached out and clamped over her mouth.

17

PHONE CALL

Herculeah remained in a state of shock. The hand was still across her mouth as the conversation in the hall continued.

"Yeah, the closet. It was the nearest hiding place. So I get through the class somehow and I come back here and I open the closet. Man, the body's gone. I mean, 'I ain't got nobody!'" He burst into song. "'How lucky can you get?'" Another song.

Then he got serious. "I figure whoever killed the guy came back and removed the body or maybe I dreamed it or maybe—hey, it's April Fool.

"Then thirty minutes ago I go out to the Dumpster

and—yeah, somebody had moved the body, but not far enough. Come on, I'll show you."

Herculeah waited, trembling, until the men's voices disappeared down the steps and out into the alley. In a burst of fright and energy, she thrust open the door.

She swerved to face—

Meat. Meat!

"You? You! What were you doing in there?" she asked.

"Same as you—hiding. I was looking around—same as you—and Mike came out to use the phone. I hid, and I was just getting enough nerve to come out when you came in."

"Do you realize how you scared me?"

"I was a bit scared myself."

"I mean, I had just realized the dead body was in the closet with me!"

"The body's out in the alley."

"Yeah, I heard."

Herculeah gave one last glance of apprehension over her shoulder at the closet door.

"Why would anybody go to the trouble of dragging a body out into the alley?"

"I don't know."

Meat's tone of voice said he didn't know and didn't particularly care.

"Are the men out there?"

Meat glanced through the glass in the door.

"Yes."

"Where's the phone? Where's the phone you were talking about?"

Listlessly Meat nodded toward the pay phone at the end of the hall.

"Money! Money!"

Meat reached in his pocket and held out a handful of change.

Herculeah made her selection.

Meat didn't ask who she was going to call. It didn't matter. Nothing did.

She told him anyway. "I'm calling my dad. I've got to get him before those clowns move the body. I've got his car phone number for emergencies."

She put in a coin and dialed.

'Dad, hi, it's me. I'm at Funny Bonz. How far away are you?"

There was a silence.

"That's good. That's perfect! Anyway, hurry. I've got a surprise for you. You remember the dead body Meat found in the bathroom?"

Another silence.

"Yes! Yes, you got it!"

She turned her delighted face to Meat. "Yes, Dad guessed it! The dead body is the surprise!" She glanced again at the door. "Now let's get back in the closet."

18

THE FACE IN THE CROWD

"Oh, Meat, come on."

He shook his head.

"Why not? You love pizza."

Herculeah was trying to get Meat to go with her and her father for a pizza.

"My dad'll drop us home right afterward. Call your mom and tell her you'll be late."

"I'm not hungry."

For once in his life it was the truth. It had been bad enough to hear Mike Howard's cruel imitation of him— to hear that stupid remark made more stupid by Mike Howard's imitation. "There's a girl in the men's bathroom"—pause, pause—"and she's dead."

But to know that Herculeah had heard it too was unbearable.

"Well, we'll drop you home."

"No."

"Oh, Meat, you ought to feel good. You were proved right. There was a body!"

Meat waved one hand in a gesture of dismissal.

"And Mike Howard and his friend have been taken downtown to give statements. Don't you want to know if they told the same story we heard? Dad can find out."

Meat shook his head.

"Meat, please."

Meat and Herculeah were sitting at a table in Funny Bonz, waiting for the investigation in the alley and men's bathroom to be finished. Being in this room made Meat feel worse. After all, it had been on that very stage where he had stood and—

Chico Jones arrived then before Meat's dreary thoughts could continue. Herculeah said, "Dad, Meat won't go with us for pizza. Make him come. Arrest him."

"I'm not hungry," Meat told Chico Jones almost apologetically.

"Dad . . ."

"Drop it, Herculeah. Meat knows whether he wants a pizza or not."

"Well, maybe he doesn't now, but when they set it down in front of us and he smells cheese and pepperoni and Italian meatballs, then he'll want it."

"You're sure you don't want to come?" Chico asked him, putting one hand on his shoulder in a fatherly, un-policemanlike way.

"Yes, sir."

"Well, don't hang around here. Go on home."

"I will."

"Want us to drop you off?"

"No."

Meat walked out of Funny Bonz with them, and after Herculeah and her father got in the car, he started for home. Chico Jones's car passed them and Herculeah honked the horn. He didn't look up.

He had felt miserable many times in his life, but he could never remember feeling quite this bad.

He was replaying that terrible moment in the closet one more time, and he was so miserable he almost didn't notice the girl who brushed against him.

He went three more steps before the realization hit him.

He spun around. "Marcie! Marcie Mullet!

She turned. Her look wasn't welcoming, but that didn't stop Meat. He felt as if he had been looking for this girl all his life.

"You don't know me, but I'm the person who found your wallet."

"Oh?"

"Yes!" He took it from his pocket.

She looked at it as if she'd never seen it before.

"Was there any money in it?"

"Some."

"That surprises me." She glanced over her shoulder. "A guy bumped against me and yanked my purse off my shoulder and ran with it."

"Well, guess where he dropped it—in Funny Bonz. That's spelled with a *z*."

"Where?"

"It's a comedy club, just down the street."

"Listen, would you mind showing me? I had some other things in my purse—some pictures and things. I'd really like to have them back. They mean a lot to me."

"I don't think there's anybody there now."

"Oh."

"The police found a body in the alley, behind the Dumpster, and they've taken Mike Howard—he owns the place—and one of his friends to the station for questioning."

Again she glanced over her shoulder. Meat looked too, but the street behind them was empty.

She shrugged. "It probably has something to do with drugs. Everything does these days. Drugs, drugs, drugs. That's all you hear."

"I guess."

"Oh, let's walk by. You can show me where it is."

Meat began to walk with her, though he didn't want to. "Oh, by the way, I went by your apartment, and I've got some bad news."

She turned to him quickly. "What?"

"Well, it looked like somebody had been in your apartment looking for something. There were clothes all over the floor and, well, it was trashed."

Now came her first smile, though it wasn't the kind of smile Meat liked to see on a girl's face. Nothing anybody would want to paint and put in a museum. "Oh, it always is," she confessed. "I keep my stuff like that. I can always find what I want."

"Oh." He was worried that he might look shocked, so he added quickly. "That makes sense."

"Show me where this place is," she said, looking at him. "What did you say the name was?"

"Funny Bonz."

"Do you have time? Do you mind?"

He did, and probably showed it.

"I wouldn't ask, but those pictures mean a lot to me."

Meat nodded. They walked in silence to Funny Bonz and tried the front door. Meat was relieved to find it was locked.

"The police must have left."

"Is there a side door?" she asked, her eyes wide with innocence.

"Yes, but it's probably locked, too."

"Just show me. I know how to get into places."

Meat walked with Marcie Mullet to the alley. She was not as tall as Meat—he glanced behind at her as she turned into the alley—but she was wider.

"They found the body over there, behind the Dumpster," Meat said.

Yellow police tape marked off the area.

"And, like I said, they took the owner and his friend down to the police station to give statements.

"This is the door." Meat tried the doorknob. "Too bad, it *is* locked."

Marcie Mullet stepped around Meat. With her back to him, she took something out of her purse and did something to the lock, and it opened with an ominous click.

"How did you do that?"

She smiled over her shoulder. "That's something my mom taught me."

"My friend's mom is a private eye, and she uses special tools."

"I use a knife." She pushed open the door.

"I don't think we ought to go inside," Meat said, but she already was. He followed, though he didn't really want to.

"You said the body was in the bathroom? Which way's the bathroom? You're going to have to show me. It's so dark in here."

Meat followed her into the hallway. He pointed down the long hall.

"I'll check." Marcie opened the door that said Guys and stuck her head inside. She looked back at Meat with real disappointment. "No, it's already been cleaned."

"Too bad about your pictures. You might check with

Mike when he—" and then he stopped.

Meat suddenly realized that he *hadn't* told her the body was in the men's room. He'd said it was in the alley. And she wasn't supposed to be looking for the body, anyway. And yet immediately she had gone to that door.

And then Meat knew.

And with the knowledge came a feeling of great power and certainty.

I, Meat McMannis, am about to solve a mystery.

This time it is I, not Herculeah, who is about to find the truth.

His feeling of power faded as Marcie Mullet started coming down the hall toward him.

And I, Meat McMannis, may not live to tell about it.

19

THE SMILE ON THE CROCODILE

"You know, don't you?"

"Know what?"

Meat tried to wipe the horror from his face and replace it with a look of innocence. "I don't know what you're talking about." His voice went up higher than he wanted it to. "I don't know anything."

"You're the one who found the body."

"Well, yes, I found the body. But that doesn't mean I know anything. You can find a body and be completely ignorant."

"I heard you coming. You were whistling," she said in a dreamlike way that for some reason made him think of somebody weird, like out of Shakespeare. Anyway, he didn't like it. "And I dragged Bennie into the stall, turned off the light, and hoped you wouldn't find him." She smiled. "But of course you did."

"Well, I couldn't help it. He fell out. I was minding my own business and he fell out. Where were you?"

"In the next stall."

"You were there?"

"Yes. I was holding my breath, praying you wouldn't open the door."

"I would never do that."

"I couldn't be sure. Finally you ran out, and I followed a little way down the hall and heard you telling everybody about what you'd found. Then that guy who owns the club came back."

"Mike."

"Yes, good old Mike." Her smile turned cruel as she said the name. "I barely had time to get out the door. I watched through the window as good old Mike dragged the body out and put it in the janitor's closet."

Meat glanced sideways for an escape and saw a blank wall. Other side, blank wall.

"Maybe he was going to get rid of Bennie's body later," she said. "He couldn't risk Bennie's body being found in Funny Bonz any more than I could."

"Why?"

"Bennie told me Mike owes big money to the wrong people, and if the club doesn't make it, he won't either."

"But why didn't you want the body found there?'

"Oh, I had reasons."

"What?"

"Because if Bennie's body was found in Funny Bonz, then the murder could be connected to me."

"How?" Meat checked again. Yes, the blank walls were still there.

"If Bennie's body was found in the club, then the police might start asking questions about why he was there and then they would ask about his routine. Did you ever hear Bennie's routine?"

"No, no, I didn't know he had one. I just saw him that one time—and I thought he was a dead girl—the purse and the ponytail and all."

"He had a routine all right." She smiled. She was a girl of a hundred smiles, and Meat didn't like any of them. "And it was all about me."

"You? You're not funny."

"No, but I'm fat."

"His routine was about fat?"

"His fat girlfriend. That was his routine—being in love with a fat girlfriend, having to kiss a fat girlfriend. 'My girlfriend has so many rolls of fat you can't tell the boobs from the tubes.'"

"But that's terrible."

"Yes, he was cruel. 'You know how bra cups come in sizes A, B, and C? Her size is WOW.'"

Meat knew that would hurt because he had seen one of those WOWs himself.

"And he was getting ready to start going all over the country with his routine. He claimed he'd get on the *Tonight Show* and *David Letterman*. And there wasn't any doubt who he was talking about—he even used my name. Mullet the Gullet. 'Restaurants have signs that say, Maximum Occupancy: 240 or Mullet the Gullet.'"

She looked at him. "You don't know how it hurts to be laughed at."

"I do, I do. Look at me."

She looked. "You're not fat."

"I am." He held his arms slightly out at his sides so she could get the whole miserable picture. And all of a sudden he was back at the newsstand, the book of fat jokes in his hand.

"Listen, I'm so big I have my own area code. When I put on my blue suit and stand on a corner, people try to drop mail in my mouth."

"Well, when I put on my yellow raincoat, people yell, 'Taxi!'"

"When I step on the scale, it goes, 'We don't do livestock.'"

"When I step on the scale, it goes, 'One at a time, please.'"

Meat swallowed, mentally flipping through the hurtful pages.

"The last time I saw *2001*, I was standing on a scale."

"My blood-type is Ragu."

"I'm so fat I eat Wheat Thicks."

Marcie Mullet seemed to be doing some mental flipping of her own.

"When I was floating in the ocean, Spain claimed me for the New World."

"I had to go to Sea World to get baptized."

"I have more chins than the Hong Kong telephone book."

"When I was lying on the beach, Greenpeace tried to push me back in the water."

They paused, both out of breath. Her eyes narrowed. "Are you making fun of me, too?"

"No, no, of myself. That was research I did for my routine at the club."

"You're not fat."

"I'm not?" A shiver of pleasure shot through his fear. "Do you mean that?"

The smile froze on his face as he saw the intent look on hers. She began to relive that terrible night.

"He had said we would talk at the club, but he pushed right on past me when I got there. He didn't even speak. I followed him inside. He went into the men's room. I even followed him in there."

Meat waited with growing horror.

"He stood by the basin. He was looking in the mirror. I was behind him. I said, 'I'm really unhappy, Benny. I'm beginning to think you don't care about me anymore.'

"He said one word. 'Anymore?'

"And the way he said that word made me realize he

never had cared. It made me realize that the only reason he went out with me in the first place was for material."

"Oh," Meat said. It was a moan of sympathy and dread.

"And then I came closer to him."

And as she said that, she came forward toward him—him, Meat!

She was moving carefully, as if she were trying to hold his attention with her eyes. Snakes did stuff like this before they struck. He glanced down and saw what was in her hand—the knife she had used to open the locked door of Funny Bonz.

He took a step backward, another. He remembered the small shiver of pleasure her compliment had given him and he tried the same thing. "Anyway, I don't think you're fat either," he lied.

"Oh, yes, I'm fat. I'm so fat that when I tripped on Fourth Avenue, I landed on Twelfth." Another smile. He hated it when she did that. "And when I play hopscotch, I go, 'New York, L.A., Chicago.'"

The way she said Chicago chilled his blood, because it was the sound of a conductor calling the absolute last stop in the world.

He tried desperately to think of one last joke to distract her. The Bermuda Triangle, what was it, exactly? Kids run around me and what? Are lost forever?

Whatever it was, Meat was never to say it. His throat had closed as if by a hangman's noose. His mouth was dry. The blood pounded in his head so hard, he couldn't hear.

And then with a smile, a strange smile that showed she was both victim and killer, she raised the knife. Then she became all killer, and the smile on her face, the last thing he knew he would see in this world, was the smile of a crocodile.

20

HERCULEAH'S HAIR

"There's something wrong with Meat."

Herculeah was beside her dad on the front seat of the car. They were on their way to Pizza House. She gave her dad a worried look.

"Well, anytime Meat turns down pizza, there's something wrong."

"I'm serious. First, I was avoiding him, because of the pictures of his dad. Now he's avoiding me."

"Meat's like a lot of people who are innocently involved in a crime. The world's not as steady as it used to be. Anything can happen. Their world's shifting beneath their feet. Meat will come around."

"Turn around, Dad! Turn around!" Herculeah said.

"We're almost there. I drove three miles out of my way because you specifically wanted Pizza House."

"Turn around."

"Why?"

"Just do it."

"I thought you were so hungry."

"I am! I was! Look at my hair!"

"What about it?"

"It's frizzling, Dad. This is the most my hair has ever frizzled in its life!"

Her father glanced at her and U-turned the car. "Where are we going?"

"Back to Funny Bonz."

"You think Meat's there?"

"My hair thinks so."

"Herculeah—"

"And I do, too."

21

A STAB IN THE DARK

Meat staggered back and found himself against a wall. He was at the end of the hall. There was a door behind him. He fumbled for the knob. Locked.

Meat was trapped.

He held his trembling hands out in front of him to ward off the thrust of the knife. The thrust would be to the heart, and he had always cared about his heart. It was the one thing that really worried him about being big—straining his heart. And now . . .

He got ready to struggle. Sure she had a knife, but he had—had what? Hands. In that split second before the stabbing, he decided it would be better to grab the knife in his hand. The hand could heal quicker than the heart. He groped for the knife, but now she was deliberately taking it out of reach.

Her arms went around him. She pulled him away from the wall. She was going for the back! She was going to stab him in the back! You could get to the heart from either side! That was why the heart was so vulnerable!

It was hopeless. And then, awaiting death, he felt something so unexpected he would have screamed if he could have.

Her arms moved up and went around his neck. What was she doing? Going for the back of the neck? Was she going to choke him?

He felt a body pressed against his. He felt cups size WOW being pressed against his chest, causing him, even in his moment of acute distress, almost to say the cup size aloud.

Then he heard the most welcome sound of his life—the clunk of something metal being dropped to the floor. He felt wetness on his neck. Tears? Could those be tears? Blood? Could she have stabbed him and he didn't feel the pain? Was he too far gone to—

"I didn't mean to do it." It was Marcie who was crying. Those were her tears. "I didn't mean to. You've got to believe that."

"I do. I do."

Meat's hands felt stupid just sticking out in the air, trembling. He rested them on her back. She was fat, but not so fat that it was unpleasant to hold her.

"I hadn't planned it. I was just standing there with my purse on my shoulder and tears rolling down my face."

"I know. I know."

"Bennie was still looking in the mirror over the basin after he said that word, *'Anymore?'* I can still hear how terrible it sounded. And then I said, 'You never did care about me?' And he said, as if he were doing me a big favor, 'Oh, at first, maybe. You were funny. You never gave a thought to your size.'

"I said, 'Now it's all I think about.'

"And then he smiled. It was kind of a nasty smile. The smile he uses on hecklers. 'Well, in case you forget,' he said, 'there's always my routine to remind you.' And he started into his routine. His routine! 'My girlfriend Mullet the Gullet is so fat, she—'

"And something came over me and I took off my purse—it had a real long chain—and I slung the chain over his head and around his neck and pulled. I just wanted to shut him up. I had to shut him up. And—and I guess I don't know my own strength."

"That happens," Meat said. "That happens."

"He just fell down, and then I heard you coming and pulled him into the stall and hid in the next one. It's just that I—like—realized what this man had done to me. I had been this happy person who liked myself and my size. I liked everything about myself, even the way I didn't have to have all my clothes folded up in neat little piles in drawers and didn't have to have my meals at exact times. And he had changed me. He had turned me into somebody different, somebody I didn't even like, and I wasn't sure I could change back."

Meat's trembling hands patted her back.

"You can. You can."

She sighed. "Anyway, I wouldn't have hurt you. You've been really nice to me. You actually seem to understand how it is."

"I do. I do."

It sounded almost like a marriage vow. Meat was discovering that if you said something twice it sounded profound, even if the sentences themselves were quite simple.

He was just getting ready to continue on the roll with a couple of *there, there*s when the side door to Funny Bonz burst open.

Meat looked up, startled. Herculeah's father rushed into the hall, his hand under his jacket on his gun. Meat's arms tightened protectively around Marcie Mullet.

Then he saw Herculeah. She was right behind her father.

Together they stared at him. Herculeah's gray eyes were thundercloud-dark and wild.

Meat barely had time to whisper two sentences, different this time, to the sobbing girl in his arms. Maybe they wouldn't comfort Marcie Mullet, but they sure sounded good to him.

"I really do understand. Once I was fat, too."

22

MACHO MAN

"So you have something to tell me," Meat said.

Herculeah sat across the table from him. The pictures of Meat and his dad were in a pile on the table, face-down. She had practiced her introduction to the pictures many times.

Now she surprised herself by saying, "I cannot believe that I was so, so worried about you—my hair was actually frizzling—and there you were hugging some woman."

"I can hug women if I want to." Despite the unpleasantness of the situation, the actual hug had been sort of enjoyable.

"And a cold-blooded killer at that."

"She may be a killer, but she certainly is not cold-blooded."

His voice had the ring of authority.

"Well, you ought to know," Herculeah said, pretending interest in the pictures.

"Is that what you called me over here for," Meat asked, "to discuss my hugging women?"

"No."

Meat could tell from her expression that it was something more serious than that. The episode with Marcie Mullet, though momentarily exciting, had left him with the feeling he'd had enough serious things to last a lifetime. This, then, was the bad news she had been putting off for so long.

Herculeah turned over some pictures from the pile in front of her. "Meat, do you remember my getting that camera from Hidden Treasures?"

"Yes, but—" He groaned. "Don't tell me you're going to show me pictures of myself. Herculeah, at this moment in my life, I'm just not up to it."

"Meat, these are pictures of you when you were probably three or four years old."

"What?"

"The camera came from your house, Meat. Your mother took the camera, along with a lot of other stuff, to Hidden Treasures. She didn't check to see if there was film inside, but there was."

He looked at the snapshots in Herculeah's hand. "Pictures of me?"

"Of you and your father."

The hand he held out was not completely steady. "My father?"

He took the pictures and spread them out in front of him. He peered down at the faces. He recognized his own—it hadn't changed that much—but his father's face . . . He didn't recognize that at all. He bent closer.

She said, "Meat." A more serious tone this time. He looked up. There were more snapshots in her hands.

"There's more?"

"Yes."

He waited. His throat was dry.

"Meat," she said quietly. She had practiced this part. "Meat, your father is a professional wrestler. He's known as Macho Man."

She kept her eyes on the pictures as she laid them out on the table, because she couldn't bear to see the disappointment on Meat's face.

She knew that he had at one time imagined his father as the conductor of a symphony orchestra, at another time as a great writer, a poet. And here he was in black leather with boots that laced to his knees and a black tattoo on each shoulder.

Meat drew the pictures closer. He slid aside those of him with his father to make room. He glanced at them one by one with an intensity that seemed to make all the goings-on in his body grind to halt. He wasn't even breathing.

"I'm sorry, Meat," she said, real regret in her voice, "but you had to know."

"Sorry?" He looked at her in amazement. "Sorry?" His eyes shone.

He glanced down. Here spread out before him was the father of his dreams—a man bigger than life—not a shoe salesman in Belks as he had once feared, not the elderly man who marked receipts with a Magic Marker at Wal-Mart. Here was a hero.

"Why didn't my mother tell me?"

"Maybe she was a—" Herculeah swallowed the rest of the word "ashamed."

"Look, did you see this one? He has his cape thrown back. He's big, Herculeah, like me, but it's all muscle."

"Yes."

"Maybe I could be like that."

"A wrestler?" she asked, trying without success to hide her horror.

"No, muscle. I mean this gives me something to shoot for. With him as my example, I can turn all this," he indicated himself, "into muscle!"

23

THE EARTHQUAKE

Meat sat between Herculeah and her dad at the Sky Dome. He couldn't believe he was here and about to see his father for the first time in years. And in action! And his father knew he was here. And! He had agreed to meet him after the show.

He had Chico Jones to thank for this wonder. One week ago Chico Jones had knocked at the front door and Meat's mother had let him in.

"Have you got a minute?" Chico had said.

"For you, Mr. Jones—"

"Chico," he reminded her.

"For you—all the time in the world."

"Good. I wanted to talk to you because I want your permission to take Herculeah and Meat on a little trip."

"Why, how nice. You know, Mr. Jones, Chico, ever since you saved my brother Neiman from that gunman, you can do no wrong in this household."

"Thank you."

"Now tell me. What kind of trip?"

Meat was hanging over the banister, listening to every word. Chico and Meat's mom moved into the living room. Meat moved down three stairs. Herculeah had alerted him to what was going on, and he didn't want to miss a word of it.

"A trip will do Albert good," his mother was saying. "He's been nervous after that horrible thing at Funny Bonz."

"I agree that a trip's in order."

"So where are you taking them?"

There was a pause. Then Chico Jones cleared his throat and said what to Meat was a beautiful word. "WrestleMania."

There followed a silence so long and so terrible, Meat closed his eyes. He could see in his mind the tight line his mother's mouth made at the mention of anything to do with his father.

"Excuse me?"

"WrestleMania . . . it's a pro . . . professional wrestling event." The expression on Meat's mother's face was evidently enough to make even a police detective stutter.

Then, while Meat's hopes sank, his mother sighed. It seemed to Meat a sign of surrender, as if all the air in her body was given up to the universe. His hopes rose.

"I guess it's time," she said.

Now Meat leaned over to Chico Jones and said, "Thanks again."

A man in a tuxedo was in the ring. "From the Sky Dome," he said, "the World Wrestling Federation welcomes you to WrestleMania!"

The crowd roared. The lights flashed. Blue lights flashed over the jam-packed arena.

Meat sat forward.

"Coming down the aisle from Baton Rouge, Louisiana, weighing in at two hundred and twenty-eight pounds is Koko B. Ware, the Bird Man!"

Music blared as the Bird Man came down the aisle. The Bird Man had a parrot on his shoulder, and he danced something that might have been the Chicken, pausing every now and then to slap hands with the fans leaning over the railing. The Bird Man slipped between the ropes and continued to dance in the ring.

"And his opponent, what a great athlete, weighing in at three hundred and twenty pounds, the Big Boss Man!"

Big Boss Man was in a policeman's uniform, beating a nightstick in one hand.

"Are you going to pull for your fellow officer?" Herculeah asked her dad.

"I haven't decided," Chico Jones said, smiling.

"I'm going to pull for the Bird Man because of Tarot," said Herculeah.

The bout itself was so quick, so violent, Meat's mouth hung open. His throat was dry.

During the next bouts, Meat got into the mood of the crowd. He booed Andrew the Giant and the Russian Tag Team. He cheered for Dusty Rhodes, the Lion King, and the Million Dollar Man. He was mad when a wrestler named Stealth stole the bag containing Jack the Snake's boa. Then, before he knew it, actually before he was ready, it was time for his father.

"And now for the championship event of the evening," the announcer said.

"Here he comes!" Herculeah said. She grabbed Meat by the shoulder. "There he is! There he is, Meat!"

"I just wish he wasn't wrestling the Earthquake," Meat said.

Then Meat saw him too, and he thought he would burst with pride.

"Now, coming down the aisle," the announcer said, "from Muscle City, U.S.A., weighing in at three hundred and seventy-five pounds, one of the longtime superstars, the World Wrestling Federation Intercontinental Champion—Macho Man McMannis!"

The music that brought his father to the ring was "Macho Man," and the crowd took it up. Meat thought, That man in the black cape and helmet and black boots laced to his knees, the man everyone is yelling Macho Man at and clapping for, is my father. Mine!

His dad stepped into the ring and threw back his cape in one motion, revealing that strong chest, those two shoulder tattoos.

The announcer said, "What a confrontation this is going to be . . . power against power with a championship belt at stake. And now, coming down the aisle, weighing in at four hundred and sixty-eight pounds is the Earthquake!"

"That's not fair." Meat was suddenly alarmed. "He's bigger than my dad."

"This guy has sent twenty-four challengers to the hospital," the announcer said, "but that's what happens when you have an earthquake!"

"Hospital?" Meat said.

There was thunder and lightning as the Earthquake entered the ring. He began jumping up and down, causing the floor to tremble so violently Macho Man almost lost his footing.

Chico Jones said, "The world hasn't seen thighs like that since the brontosaurus died out."

Macho Man went to the corner and put one foot on the ropes to check his boots. The Earthquake rushed forward and jumped him from the rear.

"Unfair! Unfair!" Meat cried. "The match hasn't even started yet."

"I think it has," Chico Jones said.

"A right over the back! There's another right! And another! Macho Man's in trouble!"

"Oh, no," moaned Meat.

The Earthquake threw himself against the ropes and knocked Macho Man to the floor. Just as Macho Man struggled to his feet, the Earthquake did it again.

"Big trouble," the announcer said.

Meat was on his feet, his hands clasped prayerlike over his heart.

Macho Man struggled to his feet, making an obvious effort to shake off Earthquake's blows. The Earthquake was strutting around the ring.

Macho Man recovered. The announcer said, "And Macho Man gets off a standing drop-kick. A back drop! What a beauty."

But then the Earthquake had Meat's father's face down on the floor, his huge knee digging into his back. The referee, slapping his hand to the canvas, was counting: "One! Two!"

Before he could give the final "Three," Macho Man twisted one shoulder free. Enraged, Earthquake pulled his father's head back, one arm around his throat. His father groaned.

Macho Man grabbed Earthquake's foot and a woman shouted, "Look out, Earthquake!" Meat glanced around in astonishment. How could anyone pull for Earthquake? That was his father! His father!

Meat turned back to the ring in time to see that Earthquake was in agony, one leg in some sort of hammerlock. Earthquake beat the floor in pain.

The announcer said, "It's a good thing that floor's reinforced!"

The crowd caught the announcer's excitement.

"Macho Man's setting him up. A beautiful back flying-drop." Earthquake fell with such force the ground seemed to tremble.

"One, two, three!" the referee counted. "It's over! The winner and still champion—Macho Man!"

He was holding Macho Man's hand in the air for victory when the Earthquake got to his feet. With a rumbling that sounded like a real earthquake, he attacked.

Within seconds, both men were out of the ring, on the floor, fighting. Other referees tried to break up the fight, but it continued up the aisle.

Meat turned to Herculeah. "He won! My dad won! He's still—what was it?" he asked Chico Jones.

"The World Wrestling Federation Intercontinental Champion."

"Yes, he's still that," Meat said.

24

THE GOTTA-GO GENE

In the dressing room, Macho Man held out his arms and
Meat went forward.

"Lemme see you. Lemme see what you look like." He
turned Meat around and studied him. His grin broad-
ened, showing two gold teeth.

"Am I glad to see you. And look at you. You're like me.
This is my boy, Al. Come meet my boy. Al here's my
manager."

"He does look like you. Hey, maybe you could form a
tag team—father and son. That's never been done."

"My boy's for better things, Al."

Meat's dad was so pleased, it was as if he'd arranged the whole thing himself. But then he said, "Ah, Albie, Albie. Thank God you found me, son. How'd it happen?"

"Herculeah . . . that's her—" Meat nodded to the doorway where Herculeah stood with her father—"she bought an old camera and it had pictures of us in it, you and me, and you were in your outfits in some, standing in front of a poster. Mr. Jones did the rest. You know about that."

His dad pulled Meat against his chest and hugged him hard. Then he pulled back for another look.

"So what's going on in your life, Albie? You keeping busy?"

"Yeah, I just solved a murder."

"Murder?"

"Yes, I found the body and then it disappeared and then I found it again and then I found the murderer." He shook his head. "Only I could never be a real detective like Mr. Jones—he's the man who brought me here—because I felt sorry for the one who did it. It turned out to be a girl. She's going to plead guilty to accidental homicide which isn't quite as bad, and Mike Howard's pleading guilty to obstruction of justice." Meat glanced over his shoulder at Chico Jones to make sure he had told it right. Chico's nod told him he had.

The Macho Man cleared his throat. "Speaking of disappearances, son," he began, "I always felt bad I left the way I did."

Meat waited.

"This doesn't justify it—nothing does—but it seems like almost every man in my family got what we call the gotta-go gene. We must have had nomads for ancestors. We can't help ourselves. One day we go out to get a newspaper or a haircut and we're outta there—just keep going. My dad dropped me off at school one morning and we didn't see him again for sixteen years."

"That's a long time to be without a dad," Meat said, speaking from experience. Ten years had been almost more than he could bear.

"I wouldn't have stayed at home as long as I did if it hadn't been for you."

Meat managed a smile. "I hope you didn't pass the gotta-go gene on to me. I like where I am."

"Well, one thing you can be sure of. Now that we found each other, son, we aren't going to let go."

He put his arm around Meat and drew him close.

"You know," Herculeah said to her father, "Meat doesn't seem bitter at all."

"You expected him to be?"

She nodded. "But then I also expected he would be ashamed that his dad turned out to be a professional wrestler." She smiled. "I guess I don't know Meat as well as I thought I did."

"Yes, he seems very proud of his father."

They looked at Meat. Pride showed in his face, in his stance. Herculeah slipped one arm around Chico Jones's waist, and she smiled up at him.

"I know the feeling," she said.

25

THE NEXT MYSTERY

Herculeah lay on her bed. It was three o'clock in the morning. She and Meat had sat in the backseat of her dad's car, talking, all the way home. She was tired. She was talked out. Yet somehow she was troubled, which really didn't make sense.

The phone rang. Herculeah knew it was Meat, so she picked up the phone on the first ring.

It woke her mother anyway. "Herculeah, was that the phone?"

"It's for me, Mom."

"Who's calling at this hour?"

"Probably Meat. I'll find out." She spoke into the phone. "Meat?"

"Yes," he whispered.

Herculeah called, "Go back to sleep, Mom. It's just Meat." Into the phone she said, "Why are you whispering?"

"I don't want my mom to hear. My mom thinks three o'clock in the morning is no time to call anybody."

"So does mine," Herculeah said. "What did your mom say about your dad?"

"About what I expected. I told her about how great Dad was and showed her his picture in the program, the one with his hands out, like he's getting ready to grab the cameraman."

"They all looked mad at the cameraman."

"True. Anyway, my mom looked at it and she got that expression she gets when she smells something bad, and she said, 'Your father may be bigger and he may have fancier clothes, but he's the same man who walked out on us and don't you forget it.'"

"Don't let her spoil it for you."

"Nobody could. It's been the greatest night of my life."

Meat waited a moment for her to answer and when she didn't, he said, "Are you still there?"

"Yes."

"Is anything wrong?"

"Oh, I don't know. I feel sort of, I don't know, dissatisfied."

"Not me. I've never felt better in my whole life."

Herculeah shifted the telephone. "You should. You found your father *and* solved a mystery."

"No, you found my father. It was a quest—like Hercules' search for the Golden Chalice."

"That wasn't Hercules."

"The Golden Fleece?"

"No."

"Well, he searched for something golden and valuable, something nobody else in the world could find. I know that much. And I know he found it! And finding my father was something no one else in the world could have done but you."

Herculeah smiled. "Your father is not golden."

Meat's voice was serious as he said, "He is to me."

"Anyway, that was an accident. I bought the camera and, let's face it, I didn't have any reason to think you and your father would be in the photos. And then it was my dad who tracked your father down. I just stood by. I hate standing by."

"No, you found my father," Meat said firmly.

"But you solved the mystery."

"Is that what's bothering you—that I solved a mystery?"

"No! Oh, maybe. I guess. Meat, there's something about solving a mystery, something about putting the last piece of the puzzle in place, that is really satisfying."

"Yes!"

She grinned into the phone. "Anyway, the next mystery is mine."

Meat realized his enthusiastic "Yes!" had come too

quickly. He thought back to the terrible parts—finding a dead body in the men's bathroom with the murderer in the next stall; hiding in a janitor's closet, alone; and then worse, with Herculeah, while a supposedly funny comic did an unfunny impression of him. And the most terrible moment of all—waiting for the knife to plunge into his heart.

He shuddered.

"The next mystery is all yours," he said firmly. There was a pause, then Meat asked, "Why are you talking about the next mystery? Herculeah, do you have one of your premonitions?"

"Well . . ."

"What? Tell me!"

"It's probably nothing."

"Tell me. Let me decide. I'm an expert on nothings."

"Remember that wrestler called the Lion King? Remember he actually roared? Remember you said his hair frizzled just like mine?"

"Yes."

"Well, when I saw the Lion King, I got a premonition."

"Lion . . . lion." Meat gasped. "The Nemean Lion! I know I'm right about that."

"Yes, I thought of that, too." She smiled. "But there are no lions around here so I'm not going to waste my time worrying about it."

"Me either," Meat lied. "Anyway," he added, more for

himself than for Herculeah, "if Hercules can overcome his lion, so can Herculeah."

"Thanks, that was nice. Goodnight, Meat."

"Goodnight, Herculeah."

And as she hung up the phone she said thoughtfully, "The Nemean Lion."

Turn the page for a preview of the newest

HERCULEAH JONES MYSTERY,

THE BLACK TOWER!

1

THE TERROR IN BLACK TOWER

Slowly she climbed the circular stairs in the tower, drawn
against her will to what waited at the top.

Halfway there, she paused. She heard the sound of the
tower door close below her. Had it been a hand that closed
it? She looked down. The thought that she might be trapped
made her dizzy.

She touched the wall to steady herself. There was an eerie
coldness to the stones beneath her hand.

She lifted her head. She listened.

She heard nothing, but she knew someone was up there,
waiting for her.

And whoever it was knew she was coming.

Slowly she took another step and another. Higher . . .
higher. With each step, her fear grew until it seemed to swirl
around her like a cape that held no warmth.

Herculeah stopped reading and let the book fall to her lap. "Are you positive this is the book you want me to read?" she asked.

The old man on the bed blinked his eyes once. That meant "yes."

"Well, I'm getting spooked," Herculeah said. "Particularly because this house, your house, has a tower attached to it. It's exactly like this one, isn't it?"

One blink. Yes.

"Have you ever been up there?"

Yes.

"What's up there? Oh, I forgot. You can't answer that kind of question. Only yes or no. Is there a room up there?"

Yes.

"Does the tower have circular stairs?"

Yes.

"That was stupid of me. I guess all towers do. Either that or they have a ladder."

Herculeah glanced out the window. She could see the tower now. It rose, black and forbidding, part of the house and yet somehow separate. Halfway up the tower there were windows. They were slits so deep in the stone that no daylight could come through.

Herculeah paused in thought. Her hands tightened on the book in her lap. The silence continued.

Herculeah had come here to read to Mr. Hunt. Her mother,

a private detective, had asked her to do this. Mr. Hunt was, or had been, one of her mother's clients.

"Why was he a client?" Herculeah had asked, instantly curious. "What did he want you to do?"

"That doesn't concern you."

Herculeah had leaned forward, more interested than ever. "What did he want you to find? That's what all old people want you to do—find someone or something from their past."

Her mother's wry smile made Herculeah think she had hit the mark.

"So what could it have been?" she went on thoughtfully. "What could have happened? Murder? Was it a murder?" Her gray eyes lit up. "It was murder, wasn't it?"

"Whatever it was happened a long time ago."

"So it was murder."

Her mother lifted one hand to silence her. "If you're going to play detective—"

"Mom, I don't *play* detective. I have solved six murders." She began to count them on her fingers. "Mr. Crewell, Madame Rosa . . ."

Her mom sighed, and Herculeah discontinued her list. "Oh, all right, what do you want me to do?"

"Just read to him for an hour or so. The man is lonely. He can't move at all since his stroke. He can only blink his eyes—one blink for yes, two for no."

"How awful! Sure, I'll do it. Actually, I enjoy reading to

people. What kind of book would an old man like? Something about old horses, old airplanes, or"—she grinned—"old women? I'll take a bunch of books so he'll have a choice. First thing tomorrow I'll go to the library and load up with books."

"Oh, there's a huge library at the house. You won't need to take anything."

"A huge library? This old man has a huge library in his house?"

Her mom hesitated a moment before she answered. "Have you ever heard of Shivers Hunt?"

"Mom! Not *the* Shivers Hunt!"

"There couldn't be but one."

"Mom, you mean I'd actually get to go inside Haunt House?"

"What?"

"Haunt House. That's what all the kids call it. And, Mom, nobody has ever been inside it. I cannot believe that I'm going to Haunt House."

"Well, you aren't going unless you stop calling it that."

"Right! Hunt House!"

"I won't let you go unless you promise you won't do anything to upset Mr. Hunt."

"I won't, I won't! I promise! But I can't help being excited. I, Herculeah Jones, am going inside"—she swallowed the word—"Hunt House."

But when Herculeah got there, she hadn't been taken to the

library to choose a book as she had expected. The nurse took her straight up the stairs to Mr. Hunt's bedroom. The book had already been chosen for her. It was waiting on the table by the old man's bed.

Herculeah picked up the book. She read the title aloud. "*The Terror in Black Tower*. This is what I'm supposed to read?" she asked the nurse.

"Yes, Herculeah. When I told Mr. Hunt that you were coming to read to him, I asked if there was any particular book he'd like. He blinked yes. I must have carried a hundred books up from the library before he finally saw this one and gave a very definite yes."

Herculeah picked up the book. On the cover, embossed in the black leather, was the silhouette of a tower. It was outlined in gold, but it looked as if someone had rubbed their fingers over the gold, as if to erase the whole tower from sight. It gave the book a sinister look. She rubbed her own fingers over the gold, then stopped abruptly.

"Well, let's get on with it." She opened the book. "Ready, Mr. Hunt?"

Yes.

Inside, the pages were thick and yellow with age. They smelled of mildew and dark passages and old secrets. Herculeah loved it.

Perhaps, she thought, Mr. Hunt had read the book as a boy,

and back then it had seemed scary, probably full of family madness and secret passages and—who knows?—maybe some terror actually had been up in the black tower.

But those things didn't exist in modern times.

They didn't.

She paused.

Or did they?

THE TRAP DOOR

Herculeah glanced at Mr. Hunt. He was waiting for her to continue. She looked down at the page.

"Where was I? Oh, yes, she's going up the tower steps." Herculeah smiled. "Actually, this will probably sound foolish to you, Mr. Hunt, but I can understand the girl doing this. I mean, she knows she's not supposed to. She knows there's something up there, something dangerous. But she can't stop herself. That's the way I am. I would do the exact same thing. The only difference would be that at this point my hair would be frizzling. I have radar hair. It gets bigger when I'm in danger. Like this."

She laughed and fluffed out her hair. Mr. Hunt watched. His bright bird eyes never left her face.

At that moment, her hair actually seemed to be frizzling on its own, as if it were anticipating the day she would climb the tower, the day she—heart racing with fear—not the character in the book, would take those circular stairs.

She patted her hair into place and said, "Oh, here's where we were." She began to read.

> Slowly she took another step and another. Higher . . . higher. With each step, her fear grew until it seemed to swirl around her like a cape that held no warmth.
>
> In the distance came the sound of thunder. She glanced out the window. She could see nothing through the dense chilling fog that circled the tower.
>
> A storm was coming. She must hurry.
>
> Still she hesitated before taking the next step. Only eight steps remained. She could see the heavy wooden door at the top now, a trapdoor.
>
> Only seven steps.
>
> Now she could hear it. The sound of breathing seemed to move from side to side behind the trapdoor. It was as if whoever, whatever was there, was trying to find a way out.

"I'm coming," she whispered.

The door to the bedroom opened behind Herculeah, and, startled, she spun around.

"Your hour's up, Herculeah," the nurse said.

"Already? I just started. I've hardly read two pages. I got

started talking about myself—I do that all the time. Plus I was getting to the good part. The girl in the book was hearing breathing. I've got to find out what's doing that breathing."

"Sorry. It'll keep. Tomorrow the print will still be right there waiting for you."

"I know." Herculeah sighed. "Actually I read a lot of books, and I've learned that authors save important things—things like what's waiting up in the tower, doing that heavy breathing—until the very end. If I know authors, this one will start a flashback just when she gets to the trapdoor. Then, on the last page—finally, finally—we'll find out what was in the tower."

"You must do a lot of reading."

"Yes."

"But we don't want to tire Mr. Hunt."

"No. Did I tire you, Mr. Hunt?"

Two blinks. No.

"But did I scare you?"

No.

She laughed. "Well, I scared myself."

Herculeah folded a ribbon into the book to hold her place. She closed the book and set it on the table.

"I'll be back tomorrow to pick up. Remember where we left off? It's getting ready to storm. The girl heard thunder. It'll be a dark and stormy night when anything can happen." She gave her words a dramatic reading.

He blinked a forceful yes.

"Dramatic things always happen during storms—though it's dramatic enough with something waiting for her at the top of the tower."

Another forceful yes.

"Do you know what's up there?"

Yes.

"Because you've read the book before?"

"Time," the nurse reminded her.

"I have to go." Herculeah smiled at the old man, his face pale against the pillows, his bright bird eyes trying to tell her something, something important.

The nurse said, "Your friend is waiting for you outside."

"Meat?"

"I think that's his name. I tried to get him to come inside, but he wouldn't."

"That's Meat."

Herculeah almost explained that Meat was afraid of this house, that he half believed the ghost stories that surrounded it, believed the stories that the portraits had holes in the eyes so that someone in a secret passage behind the wall could watch your every move.

"Meat . . . Herculeah . . ." the nurse said. "What wonderful names!"

"Meat got his because there's a lot of him. I got mine because my mom was watching a Hercules movie when she was waiting for me to be born. Mom was kidding around about naming me

Hercules if I was a boy. The nurse said, 'What about if it's a girl?' Mom said, 'She'll be Herculeah.' I guess I was lucky. The doctor got in the act and said, 'How about Samson?' He even sang it, 'Oh, Samson-ya!'" She laughed. "Anyway, everyone who knows me says it suits."

"I only met you this afternoon," the nurse said, "but I think it suits you, too."

As they moved into the hall, Herculeah said, "You know, I can't stop wondering why he chose this book." She smiled. "Although I'm always looking for the reasons people do things."

"I wondered about that, too."

"Really?"

"Because I've had other patients like Mr. Hunt, patients who have been deprived of everything but their minds. And it seems that another sense has been heightened. They seem to know what's ahead, the way an animal can sense a storm."

"Premonitions."

"Yes. If Mr. Hunt had some way of knowing there would be trouble in that tower, he would have picked this book. Well, I've got to get back to my patient."

"Right. I'll see you both tomorrow."

"Oh, I won't be here," the nurse said, smiling. "New grandchild. A Miss Wegman is taking over for me. Do you need me to show you the way out?"

"No, I remember the way."

"Because this house has a lot of halls that don't go anywhere and oddly shaped rooms. It's easy to get lost in here."

"I won't."

She started down the stairs. She was lost in thought until she glanced at the painting on the wall. It was a family portrait: old man Hunt—Lionus Hunt, who had built the house—his wife, and the four children. Mr. Shivers Hunt was the oldest of the children. Then there was a younger sister and twin girls.

Herculeah paused, half hoping to see someone peering at her through holes in the old man's eyes.

Oh, well, she told herself, it was too much to hope for.

She was turning to go when something about the twins caught her eye. The twins were dressed alike—in middy blouses—but there was something about the blouse of the smaller twin.

She bent closer. She rubbed her fingers over the painting. The figure of the smaller twin had been damaged in some way. It had been repaired, but not by the same artist who had done the original picture. Strange.

Strange, too, about Mr. Hunt's choosing the book. There was so much she didn't know, so much she would have to find out.

With a shiver of anticipation, she continued down the stairs.